ROMAN MYTHS

ROMAN MYTHS

GODS, HEROES, VILLAINS AND LEGENDS OF ANCIENT ROME

MARTIN J. DOUGHERTY

amber
BOOKS

First published in 2022

Published by
Amber Books Ltd
United House
North Road
London
N7 9DP
United Kingdom
www.amberbooks.co.uk
Instagram: amberbooksltd
Pinterest: amberbooksltd
Facebook: amberbooks
Twitter: @amberbooks

ISBN: 978-1-83886-164-3

Project Editor: Michael Spilling
Designer: Keren Harragan
Picture Research: Terry Forshaw

Printed in China

CONTENTS

INTRODUCTION

Although the power of ancient Rome came to an end in the fifth century, its influence on world culture, religion and politics continues to this day. The culture and mythology of Rome formed part of a wider narrative incorporating elements inherited from the peoples with whom Rome interacted. Arguably, Rome was not the instigator but the instrument by which this composite culture spread around the world.

As befits such a famous location, the founding of Rome is shrouded in legend. According to the mythological history of Rome, the brothers Romulus and Remus founded the city in 753 BCE. The brothers naturally have a suitably epic story. King Numitor of Alba Longa had been deposed by his brother Amulius, who wanted to ensure no claimants to the throne could be produced by Numitor's line. He forced Rhea Silvia, daughter of Numitor, to become a vestal virgin.

OPPOSITE: The tale of Romulus and Remus forms is clearly mythological, but leads into the factual history of Rome.

Rhea's vow of chastity might have prevented a conventional pregnancy, but it could not defy the gods themselves. Rhea gave birth to twin boys, naming them Romulus and Remus. The twins were fathered by Mars, god of war, and were destined to do great deeds. Although Amulius ordered them drowned in the river Tiber, the boys were found floating in a basket on the river by a she-wolf and a woodpecker. This was not coincidental; both creatures were sacred to Mars.

This founding-tale is thought to date from the fourth century BCE, well after its events supposedly took place. It reflects a number of practices common in Rome at the time, including the concepts of co-rulers and elected kings. There are other versions, in which the hero Hercules is the father of Romulus and Remus or where Amulius suspects that the boys have a mortal father. In the latter variant Amulius orders the twins to be drowned to distance himself from their murder, reasoning if they really do have a divine father his wrath might be diverted if their deaths were not by direct violence.

BELOW: **The founding of Rome has inspired artists throughout the ages. This depiction dates from 1697.**

However they came to be in the river, Romulus and Remus were saved from starvation by the she-wolf's milk and food brought by the woodpecker, and eventually adopted by a herdsman named Faustulus. Raised as common folk, the boys made good friends among the shepherds of the region, and fought alongside them in a dispute with herdsmen serving King Amulius. Remus was captured in the fighting, but was rescued by his comrades led by Romulus. Amulius was slain in the fighting, perhaps due to underestimating the combat prowess of a mere shepherd.

Although the people of Alba Longa wanted them to take Amulius's place, Romulus and

Remus instead returned their grandfather Numitor to his throne and set out to build a city of their own. This led to a dispute, with Remus selecting the Aventine Hill for the site and Romulus preferring the Palatine Hill. They agreed to settle the matter by augury, but immediately fell out over whose augury was the most favourable. Romulus reverted to type and began to fortify his location.

ABOVE: **Rome came into being due to Romulus' defeat of her first enemy – Remus, who would have built a city different in character.**

Remus responded by belittling Romulus's efforts, eventually boasting that he would jump over Romulus's walls. He did so, and subsequently died. Sources vary on exactly how this happened. Some believe that – presumably enraged at his mockery – Romulus slew his brother, or that one of his followers did so. The actual cause of death is sometimes cited as a spade thrown at Remus's head. Other versions have Remus struck down by the gods themselves, indicating they preferred Romulus's location for the city and did not appreciate his ridicule.

The new city was then constructed and soon became known by the name of its ruler. It was a cosmopolitan place, accepting almost anyone as a new citizen and thereby quickly gaining in power. A shortage of wives was addressed rather directly, as might be expected from a son of Mars. Romulus invited nearby tribes, the Sabines and the Latins, to a feast, where he took their women prisoner. This incident is commonly known as the Rape of the Sabines – in this context rape translates as 'to carry off' – and provoked conflict with the tribe.

The matter was resolved when the women of the Sabines agreed to marry their Roman abductors and asked their kinfolk not to fight. The king of the Sabines, Titus Tatius, became co-ruler of a united people alongside Romulus, and is credited with establishing altars to several gods at Rome. Within a few years

Titus Tatius was discovered to be harbouring friends who had
stolen from Rome's allies and was sent to make sacrifices in order
to win forgiveness. While he was engaged in this enterprise he
was assassinated, leaving Romulus to rule alone.

With the death of Numitor, Rome gained additional lands
and power, but the rule of Romulus was not liked by his people.
Although he had been raised among humble people, he became
increasingly elitist and authoritarian, causing considerable
dissent. Accounts of the end of his rule vary. In some he was

killed by his senators; in others he disappeared in a violent storm and was supposed by many to have become a god.

The place of Romulus was taken by a series of elected kings, until 509 BCE. In that year King Lucius Tarquinius Superbus triggered a revolt by failing to act against his son Sextus, who was accused of raping a noblewoman. His reign had been characterized by selfish cruelty up to that point, in contrast to his predecessors since Romulus. The Romans had no desire for more kings, even elected ones, and transformed their state into

a republic. The Roman republic grew into an empire-like state that dominated the Mediterranean and surrounding lands, and eventually returned to autocratic rule in 45 BCE when Julius Caesar was granted the powers of dictator for life. His adopted son Octavian, also known as Augustus, was the first emperor of Rome. At its height the Roman empire seemed invincible, conquering and imposing its values – was well as gods and myths – on an ever-increasing area. This was a two-way street, however; sometimes local gods were co-opted into the Roman pantheon. On other occasions local gods were identified with existing Roman deities, altering their nature and the stories surrounding them.

The Roman empire was entirely willing to accept new gods into its pantheon, but was resistant to the idea that there could be one true god. Thus Christianity was slow to take hold in the empire and persecution was commonplace. It was not until 313 CE that Christianity was made legal, but in 391 the empire officially

THE ROMAN EMPIRE WAS ENTIRELY WILLING TO ACCEPT NEW GODS INTO ITS PANTHEON, BUT WAS RESISTANT TO THE IDEA THAT THERE COULD BE A ONE TRUE GOD.

LEFT: Kidnapping women from the Sabines tribe turned out surprisingly well for the early Romans. Conflict was averted by the women themselves, leading to a beneficial alliance.

SOCIETY IN ANCIENT ROME

Social order was extremely important in ancient Rome. Broadly speaking, there were two main groups. The patricians were wealthy landowners, and the majority of citizens were plebians – non-nobles who might be very wealthy but lacked the social and political advantages of the patricians. Most plebians were, however, anything but rich. For much of the city's early history the plebians were largely powerless, but the balance shifted somewhat over time. The struggle for greater plebian power is known as the Conflict of the Orders. The plebians' main weapon was the need for large numbers of men to fight early Rome's wars against neighbouring tribes. While the best-equipped soldiers came from the wealthy classes, the bulk of any fighting force was made up of more basically equipped plebians. By refusing to serve in a military capacity the plebians obtained concessions that gave them a voice in government.

A Roman male was considered an adult and a full citizen once he had passed through a coming of age ceremony. This was conducted at 14–17; the exact age varied over time, though it was commonly believed that those aged under 25 were ruled solely by their emotions and tended to make bad decisions. The male head of a household had complete authority over everyone within it, and a father could choose to acknowledge a newborn child or reject it, in which case the baby would be left outside to die.

Roman society was extremely sexist, not merely refusing to allow talented women to lead or make major decisions but denying they were capable of doing so. This attitude was sufficiently ingrained that Roman writers creating accounts of distant

LEFT: From 494 BCE onward the plebian class obtained concessions by way of the secessio plebis, withholding their labour and engaging in collective bargaining with the ruling class.

lands were more inclined to believe in lands populated by men with the heads of dogs, vultures or lions than a place where women were in charge. This level of sexism coloured the perception of some cultures the Romans met, where women could hold high office and lead military forces. Such things were an affront to the Roman social order.

Ancient Rome was also a slave-owning culture, in common with most ancient societies. Many slaves were captives taken in war but others had been sold into slavery to pay a debt or raised from infancy – some of the abandoned babies left on the streets were 'rescued' in this fashion. Slaves formed the lowest of five social strata, with freedmen above them. Freedmen were, as the name suggests, former slaves who had bought themselves out of slavery or been freed by their owner. Above

ABOVE: Taking slaves to sell in the market was more than a commercial venture; it was also a demonstration of Rome's power.

them were the plebians who made up most of society. The equites (equestrians; essentially people rich enough to own horses) formed the lower part of the patrician class, with the patrician families above all others.

This social order was originally based on wealth and property ownership, but over time the balance shifted. A patrician family could suffer ill fortune and be impoverished while retaining its noble status, and many plebians gained great wealth without entering the patrician class. The social classes were separated by law in early Rome, but after 455 BCE marriage between plebians and patricians was permitted.

became a Christian state. Worship of the old gods was no longer permitted, though it doubtless continued unofficially.

Conversion to Christianity did not do away with the Roman gods and their associated mythologies. Nor did the fall of Rome. The eastern part of the empire eventually morphed into the Byzantine empire and continued for hundreds of years, but by this time it was a thoroughly Christian state and the western empire, centred on Rome itself, no longer existed. The last western Roman emperor was deposed in 476 CE, at a time when the Germanic people were in ascendance. Yet still Rome held a special place in the European psyche. In 800 Charlemagne, King of the Franks, began to style himself as emperor of the Romans. The term 'Romans' in this context had come to signify 'noble people' or 'worthy successors of the empire of Rome' rather than any specific region or population.

The term Holy Roman Empire was not applied to Charlemagne's state in his lifetime, but its successor eventually came to be known by that title. Fortunes varied over the centuries and although the Holy Roman Empire did not cease to exist until 1806 it had long since faded into irrelevance. It did, however, last just long enough to see Napoleon Bonaparte crowned as emperor of the French.

Emperor Napoleon understood the power of symbols, and none were so potent as those of the Roman empire. Almost immediately after his coronation as emperor in 1804, Napoleon dictated that regimental flagstaffs would carry an image of an eagle in the manner of the Roman legions. The first distribution of eagles to the French army took place on the Champ de Mars, dedicated to the Roman god of war. Just as

BELOW: Conversion to Christianity resulted from Emperor Constantine bargaining with the Christian god. In return for victory in battle he converted the entire empire.

in Roman times, the eagles became a powerful symbol of a force's honour and reputation. Losing a Roman eagle, the symbol of Jupiter himself, was thought to attract divine disfavour. Although Napoleon's army had no such belief, losing an eagle was a grave disgrace. Some of the most intense fighting of the era's great battles took place around these symbols.

Others have sought to co-opt the symbology of Rome. In the mid-twentieth century the Nazis grabbed every powerful symbol they could lay hands on, with some previously wholesome images now forever tainted by their association. Others have survived despite their misuse, and some may have gained an unfair reputation. The infamous 'Nazi salute' is sometimes referred to as the Roman salute, and is thought by some to derive from a Roman tradition. Although it came into use by way of Italian fascists, there is little evidence of Roman origin, the association remains all the same.

The allure of ancient Rome is not limited to politically emotive symbols. Architecture in the neo-classical style has at times been extremely popular, and even though the language of Rome is long dead it remains in use by intellectuals and academics. Latin phrases can be scattered throughout a text to make the author seem, inter alia, more erudite than a simple

ABOVE: Emperor Napoleon of France, crowned in 1804, made extensive and highly successful use of Roman symbology including the famous eagles adorning the standards of his regiments.

English equivalent. Latin mottos are common among institutions seeking a certain gravitas, and those working in science and medicine are expected to use Latin (and pseudo-Latin) to name and categorize their discoveries.

Roman associations are also commonplace in business and most other fields of endeavour. An early spaceflight programme was named Mercury after the messenger of the gods; a probe sent to Jupiter was named for the goddess Juno – his wife. Sporting contestants might be compared to modern-day gladiators, with connotations of bravery and supreme effort in the face of adversity.

Connections of this sort are evocative and therefore useful to those with something to sell – be it clothing, electronic equipment, a service or a controversial and expensive space mission. The reason these chords are struck is that Roman mythology is at least a little familiar to the average person, even today. The Roman state is long gone, but it spread its culture all over Europe, and so pervasively that it was taken to other continents as the technology of travel improved.

Yet the mythology of ancient Rome is only one part of an even bigger story. It was not created from whole cloth, but adapted

BELOW: Comparing modern athletes to gladiators is common, but perhaps rather pretentious. There are few present-day sports where participants risk being stabbed or cut to pieces.

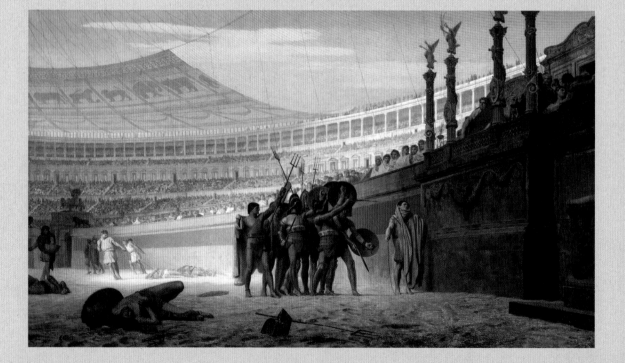

LEFT: **The Pantheon – 'Temple of the Gods', Rome. Since 609 CE the second century temple has been used as a Catholic church.**

or adopted from existing beliefs. It changed over time due to internal and external factors, and indeed continues to do so. In the modern world, Roman imagery and mythology have become mixed with other cultural symbols and concepts – notably Greek in origin but influenced by many other cultures besides.

The gods and heroes of ancient Rome are now part of what might be called a 'popular modern mythology' … but then, they always were. The evolution of myth and legend is continual and brutal. Stories are overwritten or changed to suit an agenda. They must compete against similar or wildly different myths from other cultures. They may be deliberately suppressed, or simply forgotten. That the myths of ancient Rome have survived this process is testament to their power and their ability to strike a resonance with their audience even after so many years.

DEITIES AND MAGICAL CREATURES

Roman mythology recognizes a range of powerful beings. The most potent are the major gods, followed by a host of minor deities associated with specific places, functions or concepts. Some god-like beings are not accorded the status of deities and may be referred to as Titans. This does not necessarily mean they are less powerful than the gods themselves, but they are not part of the main group and generally not worshipped.

A host of lesser beings also exist. Powerful spirits are often referred to as nymphs, though the distinction between a nymph and a minor god is blurry at best. Other creatures may be thought of as a sort of magical species, such as fauns or centaurs, or individual beings. These include monsters such as Python or small groups such as the Furies, which might in some cases be a subset of nymph-like beings.

1

THE HISTORY AND MYTHOLOGY OF ROME

For more than two thousand years Rome has played an important part in European and world politics and culture. From a small city-state it grew to be the heart of an empire, fell to barbarians, and rose again as the capital of a modern nation. The city has seen empires and states rise and fall, always enduring. For this, Rome earned the nickname The Eternal City.

The earliest presence of humanity's ancestors in what is now Italy is thought to date from around 850,000 BCE. There is some debate about the arrival of Homo Neanderthalensis and Homo Sapiens, due to the difficulties of dating some evidence, but it is quite possible that a human population was present around 210,000 BCE. There is evidence elsewhere of a gradual spread through the Mediterranean islands and nearby coastal areas, occurring much earlier than previous estimates.

OPPOSITE: Even after more than two millennia, the grandeur of the Colosseum and the Forum in Rome still endure.

These populations are likely to have been the result of small-scale migration – the wanderings of families and tribes rather than a large-scale movement. Groups would settle where conditions were good, with later arrivals joining existing communities or pushing on in search of land of their own. It was not until around 60,000 BCE that Homo Sapiens began moving out of Africa and settling elsewhere in large numbers.

These migrations took place against the backdrop of the Last Ice Age, which had profound implications for early humanity. Human and animal populations, as well as regional climates, were affected in a variety of ways by the increase in glaciation leading to the Last Glacial Maximum. This occurred around 21,000–22,000 years ago, with a series of glacial advances and retreats taking place before and after the maximum coverage was reached. On the one hand sea levels were much lower, which facilitated movement between land masses, but at the same time dry conditions rendered many land areas unviable.

The ice sheets themselves were uninhabitable, other than by hunting parties using small boats to move along the edge of the

LEFT: Petroglyphs pecked out by striking a stone against another prove that early humans were capable of abstract thought and expression.

ice shelf. Other areas might be useable for a time then dry up or become threatened by rising sea levels. Changing rainfall patterns and temperature conditions were other factors driving migration of early human populations. In some cases this was the direct result of changing conditions; in others secondary factors were in play, such as the spread of vegetation to a previously arid area.

The retreat of the glaciers was rapid – in geological terms, at least – once it began, possibly causing mass extinctions and certainly putting animal populations under pressure. As sea levels rose, human groups were cut off from other land masses or forced to move inland. Others ventured into the new territories that were opening up as the glaciers retreated, or adapted to changing conditions as forests became savannah and arid regions started to receive adequate rainfall.

There are, of course, no written records from this period, but humans were anatomically and behaviourally modern at this time. Capable of abstract thought, the people of the early post-Glacial Maximum period expressed themselves through art and no doubt discussed the great questions of how and why their universe worked as it did. Carvings and cave art tell us a little about how these people thought and felt, and we are able to reconstruct a reasonable picture of how they lived. Although lacking in technology, the people of the time were smart and inquisitive – and entirely capable of solving problems by making devices using the materials they had to hand.

Advancing technology

The earliest tools used by humanity's ancestors were chipped from suitable stones or simply picked up from the ground. Antlers, bones and the like sufficed as picks or levers. This level of tool use spanned the period from the beginnings of humanity

ABOVE: **A spear head dating from prehistoric Italy, ninth–seventh centuries BCE.**

MYTHICAL HISTORY AND POPULAR MYTHOLOGY

The early history of Rome is what might be termed a 'mythical history', with obviously mythological events and individuals presented as historical figures. At some point the characters and occurrences become verifiably real, but there may still be a mythical element. Since many Roman figures claim descent from their gods, it is arguable that any event in the entire history of Rome has a mythological element.

Later writers may have ascribed mythical connections to real people, or assumed that a mythological figure was in fact real. There is also significant interplay between beliefs and events. A lost battle might be ascribed to poor auguries before the attack. This can seem fanciful to the modern reader, but to the people of the time a set of inauspicious omens might reduce morale and genuinely affect the outcome of a conflict.

The history of Rome also gives us a great variety of figures of speech and references to people and events that, although historical rather than mythical, have passed into a sort of modern cultural pseudo-mythology. When military forces attempt to bring about a battle of annihilation by double envelopment of the enemy's flanks, they are often said to be recreating the Battle of Cannae (216 BCE). A costly victory is a 'Pyrrhic victory'.

Although these are historical events, much of what we know about them comes from the writings of people who believed in the mythology of the time, and those beliefs may well have influenced their view of what was fact and what was myth. It is thus almost impossible to separate the history and mythology of Rome. The people of the time certainly had no interest in doing so.

BELOW: **The battle of Cannae in 216 BCE has become a byword for a double-envelopment attack crushing the flanks of an opposing army.**

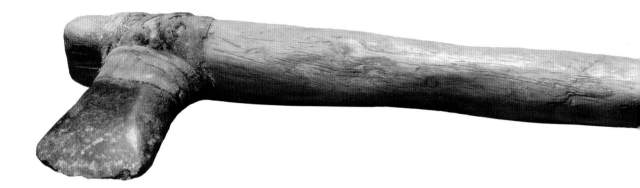

to around 10,000–8,000 BCE. After this, technology advanced at an increasing pace, with more complex tools gradually appearing. These included cutting tools created by fixing small fragments of chipped stone to a shaft, and permitted more complex work to be undertaken as well as more efficient gathering of food.

This move towards more advanced technology occurred at different times and places in differing locales, and was accompanied by a change in lifestyle. The implementation of agriculture both necessitated and facilitated a movement to fixed settlements rather than a nomadic lifestyle. Improvements in food production and storage allowed the rise of specialized crafters, who had the skill and could take the time to produce higher-quality stone tools. These, in the right hands, improved prosperity and were valued as trade items.

High-quality tools and weapons became status symbols, in the sense that someone who possessed such items was a friend worth having – or perhaps worth cultivating. Better tools translated into increased ability to generate wealth, or at least get enough food, hopefully enabling the rich individual to assist those of whom they thought highly. Other status symbols were more abstract. Possession of highly decorated items – for example, using colourful seashells – did not make the individual any more capable of directly generating wealth but symbolized their ability to do so, and perhaps created a secondary route to greater prosperity.

Those hoping to win favour might present the wealthy individual with gifts, further increasing their personal wealth. As the means to gain prosperity developed, so social strata

ABOVE: **The manufacture of stone tools was a mature technology, with well-made examples prized as trade goods all across Europe.**

could begin to emerge, which were based on possessions rather than skills or physical attributes. Where previously only the abilities of an individual as a leader or provider of high-level skills counted towards social status, now possession of objects – gained by whatever means – was a factor. Long before the development of civilization, some of its attributes were already beginning to appear.

The use of metal began with copper, which is found in its native state and can be extracted by chipping away the surrounding stone. The softness of copper enabled the first metalworkers to pound it into shape, but also limited its usefulness as a material for toolmaking. Mixing molten copper with tin produced bronze, the first metal capable of fully supplanting stone for toolmaking.

Metalworking was made possible in part by a sedentary lifestyle based on agriculture, and as it required significant equipment, reliance on metalworking also forced the adoption of a static way of life. The move towards more advanced communities was thus self-reinforcing, and with it came changes in the construction and organization of settlements.

BELOW: **The production of metal tools like these bronze axe-heads was facilitated by a move to a more sedentary lifestyle, leading ultimately to the rise of cities.**

From around 4500 BCE, copper and then bronze tools became increasingly prevalent in the northern Mediterranean region. This was not a uniform progression; some regions experienced a distinct 'copper age' whereas others seem to have progressed almost immediately to bronze-working. In most cases the use of metal existed alongside advanced stone tools for many years. Early metal objects were small, such as hooks and fasteners, though this had a lot to do with the relative ease of fashioning them from metal and the difficulty of making larger items.

Overall, stone tools were perfectly adequate for most roles and were a well-established, mature technology. There was simply no need for a replacement, meaning that metal was valued initially for its new applications. In time, however, the advantages of metal caused stone to be supplanted. Likewise, the move from a nomadic lifestyle to a fully sedentary one was not immediate. Many communities acted as a base for hunting or gathering parties as well as conducting agriculture and raising livestock. Initially, animals appear to have been kept almost purely for meat, but in time their value as power sources for ploughing and transport became apparent, along with a rise in the use of secondary products such as milk and eggs.

Initially, most tasks such as the creation of pottery were undertaken on a household basis, but, just as with metalworking, the more settled lifestyle of the era permitted the rise of specialists. These required the support of food-producers, which in turn necessitated a more organized society. Inevitably, a recognizable social hierarchy began to develop.

The Italian Bronze Age

The technology of the Bronze Age was in no way primitive. Metalworkers could produce tools to suit almost any need, along with intricate designs in gold and silver for decorative purposes. As the technology of bronze matured, better and lighter tools increased efficiency and permitted further economic specialization. The Bronze Age in Italy dates from around 2300 BCE to perhaps 900 BCE, and is subdivided into segments whose dates and identity vary depending on the source consulted.

There is evidence that as the Bronze Age progressed, increased use of fortified settlements became the norm. However, it is not clear whether the fortifications served a purely military purpose or were intended to facilitate greater economic and political control over the population. These settlements did not exist in isolation, and were connected to one another by local

ABOVE: Rome's earliest armies fought with bronze-tipped spears, in a style reminiscent of Etruscan forces.

routes as well as long-range trading expeditions around the coasts of the Mediterranean.

Around 1200 BCE, the Bronze Age civilizations of the eastern Mediterranean came under pressure from a threat referred to as the 'sea peoples'. The identity of these people, and even whether they were a single group or many, remains unclear. What is known is that the Mycenaean Civilization, which dominated much of Greece and the surrounding islands, collapsed and

cities all around the eastern end of the Mediterranean were sacked. This brought about what is known as the Greek Dark Age and severely disrupted trade in the region.

One consequence of the collapse of Greek civilization was an impetus to move to ironworking. The people living north and west of Greece, known to the Greeks as Keltoi (essentially, 'barbarians'), obtained most of their tin by way of trade. With this source disrupted it became difficult to make bronze. Iron offered an alternative, and ironsmithing became a developing technology. The first iron tools and weapons were no better than those made from easily worked bronze, so up to this point there had been little reason to explore the possibilities offered by iron.

Once it became necessary to start working iron the technology rapidly matured, to the point where iron items were notably superior to those made with bronze. As Greece emerged from its dark age and began exporting tin once more, there was little need to return to using bronze. However, bronze and iron were in use side by side for many years.

LEFT: The sea peoples were generally successful in their campaigns, but were defeated by Egyptian naval forces under Ramses III at the Battle of the Delta (1175 BCE).

The Iron Age

Italy is considered to have entered the Iron Age around 800 BCE, at a time when civilization was reawakening in Greece and elsewhere in the eastern Mediterranean. The cities of Phoenicia, in what is now Lebanon and the surrounding middle eastern countries, had become enormously prosperous through trade and were establishing colonies as forward trading posts as far afield as

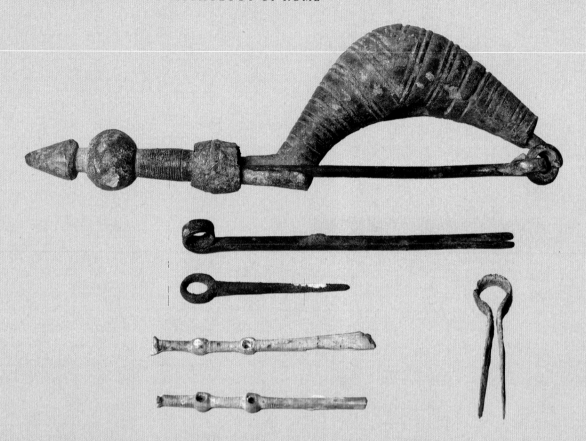

ABOVE: Iron Age tools found at Golasecca, in the Po Valley. The Golasecca culture developed in the late Bronze Age and progressed to iron working over time.

modern Spain and Tunisia. There, the trading port of Carthage would eventually become a power in its own right and challenge Rome for supremacy in the western Mediterranean.

Greek city-states were also beginning to emerge, fighting one another or creating political alliances as circumstances dictated. Greek expeditions founded colonies and outposts along the shores of the Mediterranean, establishing a major presence in southern Italy. The first Greek colonies in Italy were established around 740 BCE at Cumae, with many others following. Greece was not at that time a nation or an empire, but a place with a generally common culture among its city-states. Some of these dominated territories that might be considered a state, but overall the Greek world was one of city-states and their possessions rather than any sort of unified polity.

The people of Italy

Iron Age Italy was populated by a variety of peoples who had arrived by different routes over the centuries. Waves of large- and small-scale migration had taken place for thousands of years, creating an indigenous population that was swelled by new arrivals. These new arrivals came mainly from the east, and are generally referred to as Indo-Europeans. They brought with them a language family that came to dominate European speech, and a proto-Indo-European religion.

The new arrivals found people already in Italy and elsewhere. Some of these groups can be considered indigenous, since they had been present for millennia. Others may have spread eastwards from the Iberian Peninsula. The origins of these people are largely unclear, but they are typically referred to as non-Indo-Europeans. They had their own languages, beliefs and traditions, which mingled with those of the new arrivals to create what would ultimately become 'Roman' culture.

Among those arriving from the east were the Iapyges, who migrated into eastern Europe from around 2500 BCE. They spread westward north and south of the Alps. Those who went south initially settled in Illyria and northern Italy, where their development was influenced by contact with the Greeks. Those who settled north of the Alps and in the north of Italy are considered to be the ancestors of the Keltoi, or Celts. This is all a

BELOW: Two of these gold leaf sheets bear writing in Etruscan, whilst the third is in Phoenician. They date back to the sixth century BCE.

very broad generalization, of course. There were no neat and tidy tribal or cultural definitions, and the identity of any given group is debatable.

Over time, the Iapyges migrated into southeast Italy and became one of the components of the general group referred to as the Italics. Their language was descended from the proto-Indo-European language, and it is entirely possible they brought with them beliefs and stories that found their way elsewhere during other migrations. Proto-Indo-European populations entered India and reached Scandinavia, suggesting that similarities with the mythologies of these areas might not be entirely coincidental.

The culture of the Italic tribes was heavily influenced by that of Greek colonies in Italy. This is not exactly the same thing as being influenced by 'Greek culture', as there was in reality no such thing except in the broadest possible terms. The culture of a given colony was a mix of local customs and those of its parent city in Greece, and since both of these varied the influence on the Italic tribes living close by produced differing results. Indeed, the culture of the Italics influenced the Greek colonies to some extent, though it is likely the parent Greek city-state's values were dominant.

The primary Italic tribes were the Umbri, who settled in the region today known as Umbria, the Osci who dwelled south-west of them and the Latins of central Italy. Their language would eventually come to be the standard throughout the Roman world, but in the early Iron Age the Umbri and the Osci spoke different tongues.

In the south of the Italian Peninsula, the dominant tribal group was the Samnites, or Sabines, who spoke the same language as the Osci, and to the north dwelled the Etruscans. Their origins are particularly unclear, but it is known that

BELOW: Earthenware vessels of this sort were in use by the Etruscans in the eighth century BCE, at the time when Rome is traditionally said to have been founded.

they had a complex society by the seventh century BCE. Etruscan towns developed into cities, heavily influencing the development of Roman society. The Ligures, dwelling in northwestern Italy and Corsica, appear to have been an indigenous European population overlaid by Indo-Europeans.

For the most part the territories of these tribes were delineated by natural barriers such as rivers and mountains. Smaller groups held territories between or sometimes within those of the larger tribal confederations. Among these were the Veneti, who possibly took control of the area around 1000 BCE after migrating from Illyria. The Veneti traded over a wide area and had strong links with Greece.

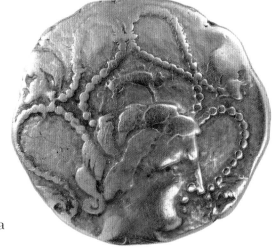

ABOVE: A gold coin of Veneti or perhaps Namneti origin, dating from the second century BCE. The tribes of Italy traded widely, often with Greek city-states, and absorbed Greek culture along the way.

The founding of Rome

One version of the founding of Rome has legendary heroes deciding to build a city to rule, but there are other stories besides. Writing around 30–20 BCE, the Roman poet Publius Vergilius Maro (70–19 BCE), better known to history as Virgil, told a tale linking ancient Rome to the Trojan War of ancient Greece. The latter is known mainly from the work of the Greek poet Homer, writing around 750 BCE.

In his Iliad and Odyssey, Homer tells of a war between the Greeks and the Trojans, instigated by divine interference in human affairs. The 10-year siege of Troy ends with its destruction. Long thought to be fictional, it is probable that the tale of Troy derives from oral traditions dating from before the Greek Dark Age. Homer was writing around 750 BCE, as the Greek civilization began to recover from the Bronze Age Collapse. The ruins of a city in a suitable location, sacked at about the right time, provide some evidence that Homer's work is derived from older stories.

Be that as it may, among the many characters in the *Illiad* is the Trojan Aeneas, who becomes leader of the survivors after the fall of Troy. His followers leave in ships, having many adventures around the Mediterranean. Virgil's *Aeneid* tells the tale of Aeneas

IT WAS THE JEALOUS KING AMULIUS OF ALBA LONGA WHO TRIED TO KILL ROMULUS AND REMUS, THEREBY SETTING THE STAGE FOR HIS OWN DESTRUCTION AND THE FOUNDING OF ROME.

and is the inspiration for the opera Dido and Aeneas. Dido was a queen of Carthage, where Aeneas and his followers stayed for a time, but ultimately he landed in Italy.

Aeneas's journey was instigated by the hero Hector, who chose to save some part of Troy's greatness from destruction. Aeneas was divinely guided to the location where he finally settled, and when he fell in love with Dido and considered staying at Carthage, the god Mercury intervened to set him right. Aeneas' dutiful obedience to divine command is lauded as a great virtue by Virgil, though Dido committed suicide on being abandoned.

It is likely that Virgil wove several legends about Aeneas together to create his version. Aeneas is very much a Roman culture-hero – not only is he a devoted servant of the gods but also an enemy of the Greeks. The legend of Aeneas founding Rome also provided a link to Troy, one of the most famous cities of mythical antiquity, and added to the gravitas of the Roman heritage.

According to Virgil, Aeneas made friends with King Latinus on his arrival in Italy, and a marriage alliance was agreed. When this broke down Aeneas and his followers had to fight the Rutuli tribe and, on their victory, he married Latinus's daughter Lavinia. His story is not incompatible with the tale of Romulus and Remus – Aeneas founded a city named Lavinium, and his son Ascanius in turn founded Alba Longa. It was the jealous king Amulius of Alba Longa who tried to kill Romulus and Remus, thereby setting the stage for his own destruction and the founding of Rome. In some versions of Aeneas's tale, his followers decide they do not wish to sail any further and take wives from among the local women. In others, they have their wives with them and it is the women who decide the voyage is over. The argument caused by this decision is resolved when the women burn Aeneas's ships, forcing his followers to make the best of where they have landed. This is the location upon which Rome now stands.

The tale of Romulus and Remus, and the *Aeneid*, form what

BELOW: **The tragic tale of Dido and Aeneas has inspired music and art for centuries. This depiction, dating from 1815, is by Pierre-Narcisse Guerin.**

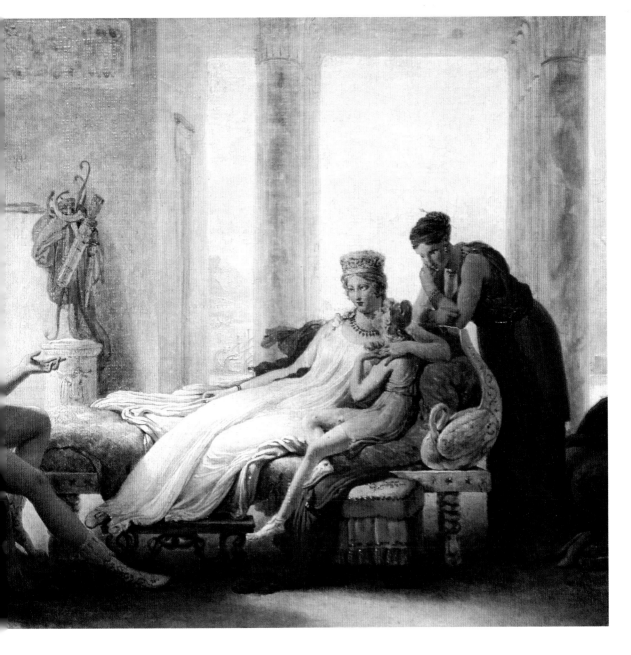

termed a mythical history of the city. This provides links to ancient Troy and to the gods themselves. The reality of Rome's founding may be a little more mundane, however. It is probable that the city originated in multiple villages that grew together into a town and finally a city. Early society was heavily influenced by the Etruscan culture, which had developed into a loosely organized league of city-states.

The city's military strength was organized along similar lines to that of the Etruscan city-states, who in turn had adopted Greek practices. Warfare was the responsibility of all citizens, who had to provide their own arms and equipment. The war gear a man could afford delineated his status in society. The richest fought on horseback, with heavy infantry armed with long spears provided by the next echelon, and similarly armed lighter

BELOW: Ferdinand Bol's depiction of Aeneas at the court of king Latinus dates from around 1661–63. The distinctly 'Roman' armour of the main figures is anachronistic.

infantry by the social class below. The poorest citizens fought as skirmishers or missile troops. This model worked well enough for local disputes, though Greek-style heavy infantry armed with long spears were not well suited to mountainous regions.

ABOVE: The image of Romulus and Remus being suckled by a she-wolf is one of the most instantly recognisable in Western culture.

Monarchy to Republic

Until 509 BCE, Rome was ruled by a succession of kings. These were elected by the senate and were not descended from any particular ruling line. Records are scarce, but among the early kings of Rome were Etruscans, including Tarquin the Elder (Lucius Tarquinius Priscus), who reigned from 616 BCE to 579 BCE.

Tarquin the Elder may have been culturally Etruscan, but he was the ruler of Rome and put her interests first. A successful

campaign in Etruria drew in a response from all over the Etruscan
League, which was defeated by Tarquin's army. There appears
to have been no large-scale conflict with the Etruscan cities
for some time, though skirmishing and local disputes will have
occurred. Tarquin the Elder was succeeded by Servius Tullius
(reigned 578–535 BCE), who is variously claimed to be an

Etruscan or a Latin. Servius Tullius is credited with implementing a five-tier social system organized according to the wealth of the individual, though many details from this period are vague at best. In 535 BCE he was killed by his daughter and her husband Lucius Tarquinius Superbus (Tarquin the Proud; reigned 534–510 BCE), who was then elected king.

Tarquin the Proud was, by all accounts, a tyrannical and despotic king. He had several senators put to death for opposing him, and ultimately alienated his people to the point where his family were driven out of the city. The flashpoint for the revolt was the rape of Lucretia, a well-respected noblewoman, by Tarquin's son Sextus. Tarquin made allies among nearby Etruscan cities, resulting in a period of conflict, but was unable to regain his throne.

After Tarquin the Proud there were no more kings in Rome, and a distinct distaste for them. Rather than a single ruler, even an elected one, politico-military power – known as imperium – was granted each year to a pair of co-ruling consuls. Consuls governed in all matters, and each could veto any decision made by the other. Politics and military leadership went hand in hand throughout the history of Rome, with little distinction between the two. On the other hand the former religious duties of the king were carried out by a 'sacred king' or Rex Sacrorum, who held the office for life.

The development of Rome during the early republic followed a pattern common in Greece as well as Italy. Rome itself was a city-state, but held territories and colonies giving access to greater resources than those immediately available

OPPOSITE: **Attius Navius declared he could read Tarquin the Elder's mind, and Tarquin stated he was thinking Attius could cut a whetstone in half with a razor. Attius promptly did so, though in this late 1600s depiction he is cutting a column.**

BELOW: **Titian's early 1500s depiction of Tarquinius and Lucretia shows Tarquinius as a rather sinister figure, though it was his son Sextus who was accused of her rape.**

to the city. Beyond these immediate holdings Rome built a network of alliances and treaties enabling her to field much greater forces than a single city-state might.

Early conflicts

Rome's first conflicts were small and localized. Some were fought against nearby tribes, largely over territory, and few records survive. Much of what is 'known' about these conflicts today is mythology as much as history. It appears that the series of conflicts known as the Etruscan Wars began in 483 BCE with an inconclusive campaign against the Etruscan city of Veii. The war was characterized by low-level raiding and the occasional larger clash, resulting in a treaty in 474 BCE.

Conflict resumed in 437 BCE, by which time Etruscan power had been greatly reduced by clashes with Greek forces. Another truce ensued, requiring Veii to pay tribute to Rome. Failure to do so was a pretext for another clash, and in 396 BCE Veii became a Roman possession. In 358 BCE Rome came into conflict with Tarquinii, another Etruscan city. Characteristically of this period, aid from other Etruscan city-states was slow to arrive, if it came at all. More unified action came in 311 BCE, when several Etruscan city-states formed an alliance.

The growing power of Rome was such that even while engaged in warfare against the Samnites, Roman forces were able to subdue the Etruscan cities and force treaties on them. Over the next three decades, formerly Etruscan cities became allies of Rome, assisting against the Gauls. By the end of the Etruscan Wars, Rome was the dominant power in the region. However, this was achieved only at the price of major social changes. By the end of the Etruscan Wars the plebian social class had obtained a share in government.

In addition to wars with the Etruscans, Rome – and other city-states – came under threat from the Celtic tribes of northern Italy. Known collectively to the Romans as Gauls, these tribes included the Senones. It is likely that this tribe was part of a larger group that split, some elements taking possession of lands

ABOVE: The statuette, dating from the fifth century BCE, depicts a warrior in a crested helmet. He may have originally been holding a shield in his left hand.

in northern Italy while others continued west and settled on the Seine. These 'other Senones' came into conflict with Rome in the last years of the republic, and indeed were part of the events that led to the transition to empire.

The Senones of northern Italy arrived there around 400 BCE, taking land from the Umbrians and pushing southwest. Reaching Clusium, they laid siege to the city. Clusium was an Etruscan city that had previously fought against Rome, but this new invasion threatened all cities in the area. Rome responded to the call for aid and sent a delegation to negotiate with the Gauls. The delegates quickly realized there was nothing to be gained by diplomacy, and although Rome had little interest in helping Clusium, it was in her interests that the Gauls be defeated.

The delegates encouraged the Clusians to fight and joined them when they did. This was a major diplomatic gaffe because the delegation had arrived under safe passage as emissaries of

BELOW: **Publius Horatius Cocles is credited with saving Clusium by defending a narrow bridge until reinforcements arrived. This deed is still a figure of speech today.**

peace. The Gauls demanded the delegates be handed over for justice, which was refused. Thus Rome accidentally assisted Clusium by drawing the wrath of the invaders against herself. The Gauls raised the siege of Clusium and marched against their new enemy.

The leader of the Gauls, a war-chief named Brennus, is part of the mythical history of Rome. He may well not have existed at all, but some surviving sources refer to an individual by this name and he has become a semi-historical figure. Whoever was leading them, the Gauls were able to defeat a Roman army in the field at the battle of the river Allia. Most of the Roman army was destroyed in this disastrous encounter, and on arriving at the

BELOW: A stealthy attack by Gaulish warriors was foiled by noisy geese, preventing the fall of the Romans' last stronghold.

city the Gauls were able to capture most of it without significant resistance. Some defenders held out on the Capitoline Hill, where they were besieged.

According to legend, the Gauls attempted to break the siege with a surprise assault, which very nearly succeeded. They were able to do so because the city's dogs did not bark in warning. The wily Gauls had thrown food to the hungry dogs, which were occupied in filling their bellies and unconcerned about the advance of their benefactors. However, the temple geese proceeded to make a tremendous noise, rousing the defenders. As a result, an annual sacrifice was implemented, named Supplicia Canum, in which dogs were ritually crucified and geese lauded as heroes.

THE LEADER OF THE GAULS, A WAR-CHIEF NAMED BRENNUS, IS PART OF THE MYTHICAL HISTORY OF ROME.

The legend of Brennus further states that Rome agreed to pay tribute to the Gauls, but a dispute arose because the measures in use differed. Brennus's solution to this problem was to throw his sword on the scales alongside the Gauls' weights and announce 'woe to the vanquished!', suggesting that quibbles over the precise weight of silver offered in tribute might not be advisable.

The Gauls were subsequently defeated by a force raised from nearby cities, and Brennus disappears from the historical record. If he existed at all he was presumably killed in the Gauls' defeat. The architect of this victory was Marcus Furius Camillus, who had led a successful campaign against Veii but subsequently

ABOVE: Brennus is one
of several probably-
mythical figures
intertwined with Rome's
history. He is probable
a conflation of several
Gaulish leaders.

went into voluntary exile. Despite – or perhaps because of – his
obvious talents as a soldier and a statesman, his enemies accused
him of misconduct and colluded against him.

The lack of a leader of Camillus's calibre was obvious at
the battle of the Allia, where the over-confident Roman army
failed to make the correct military and religious preparations
for battle. Deployed badly, with no field defences in place, the
army also neglected to perform the necessary sacrifices and was
subsequently trounced. Only when Camillus agreed to return
from exile and lead the relief of Rome were the Gauls driven off.

Camillus was lauded as the 'second founder of Rome' or
the 'second Romulus', but differs from the first in that there
is archaeological evidence of his deeds. He personifies the
dedicated servant of the state, a very Roman ideal, and also
the 'competent man' who stands above others by virtue of his
talents and good decisions. As such, he passed into the cultural
mythology of Rome.

The sack of Rome had a profound effect on Roman culture and outlook. In addition to drawing attention to the foolishness of neglecting the proper sacrifices, defeat at the Allia exposed the dangerous weaknesses of the Roman military system. No longer were distant barbarians discounted as a threat – Roman citizens had felt the terror of foreign warriors plundering their homes, and began to view external threats with far less complacency.

First among equals

Rome did not control other cities in the manner of an empire or kingdom. Instead she was the leader of an alliance, the 'first among equals' – at least in theory. In practice the economic, military and political power of Rome was such that she wielded immense power over her allied city-states even if she did not command them directly. Any city that opposed the will of Rome was likely to encounter opposition from others – all carefully orchestrated by the expert statesmen of Rome.

If economic pressure and the threat of military action were not enough, Roman and allied forces were quite capable of overcoming most resistance. The Latin War of 340–338 BCE saw Rome pitted against an alliance of Latin cities that resented her dominance of the Latin League. This threat was swiftly crushed, but the Samnites of central Italy proved more of a problem. They were only subjugated after three wars in 343–341 BCE, 327–304 BCE and 298–290 BCE.

This expansion did not take place in isolation. In 336 BCE, King Philip II of Macedon (382–336 BCE) was succeeded by his son Alexander, who soon earned himself the title 'the Great' by creating an empire covering Greece, Persia, parts of Egypt and even

BELOW: The first battle of the Latin War was fought near Mount Vesuvius. Both Roman commanders dreamed that victory would come only if one of them died, causing Consul Publius Decius Mus to make a suicidal attack and thereby ensure a supernatural advantage.

reaching India. Macedonian ascendance did not greatly trouble Rome, and was in any case short-lived; Alexander's death in 323 BCE resulted in division of his empire, which rapidly fragmented further.

The collapse of the Macedonian empire was probably fortunate for Rome, but it did leave various Greek successor states, which retained considerable power. Most influential on the affairs of Rome was the domain of King Pyrrhus of Epirus (319–272 BCE). His ambition was to build an empire of his own, which included the Greek territories in Italy, and this meant opposing the expansion of Rome wherever possible. Conflict between Rome and the Greek colony at Tarentum resulted in intervention by Pyrrhus, bringing about the Pyrrhic War of 280–275 BCE.

Costly victories over Roman forces in Sicily earned Pyrrhus a dubious connection with heavy casualties – the 'Pyrrhic victory' – but in fact he was an able strategist who proved a major threat to Rome. However, after being distracted by campaigns against Carthaginian territories and bogged down against Roman-led forces that could replace losses the Greeks could not, Pyrrhus retreated from Italy and allowed Rome to take control of what had been Magna Graecia.

Roman expansion continued, and with it the gradual Romanization of controlled territories. Individuals who had served as consuls were typically given a governorship afterwards. Many saw this as nothing more than an income source and ran their territory accordingly, though some took a longer view and were more moderate in their self-enrichment. Closer links with Rome, along with the settlement of traders and artisans in the new territories, resulted in changes to the local culture. This was to some extent a two-way street. Rome acquired elements of the cultures it absorbed, but for the most part the effect was to export Roman religion and social values.

Expansion brought about conflict with the other powers of the Mediterranean world. Lying between Italy and Carthage, and also with a strong Greek presence, Sicily was an inevitable flashpoint. Carthage had grown from a Phoenician trading colony into a major power in its own right, and sought to control the

OPPOSITE: **The battle of Heraclea in 280 BCE was a 'Pyrrhic Victory' for the Greeks under King Pyrrhus of Epirus. Heavy losses made the campaign unsustainable despite victory in the field.**

surrounding seas. To contest the Mediterranean, Rome had to learn to fight at sea, and set about building a fleet to do so.

Roman maritime warfare in this period lacked the artistry of Greek or Carthaginian manoeuvring. Instead the Roman galleys sought to grapple their enemies and bring about a boarding action. This proved sufficient, and in the First Punic War of 264–241 BCE Roman forces gained control of Sicily and Corsica. Operations on land against Carthage herself went less well, however.

Seeking gains to offset her territorial losses, Carthage turned her attention to the Iberian Peninsula. This inevitably led to further conflict because Rome also had ambitions in the region. During the Second Punic War of 218–201 BCE, Carthaginian power was broken and Rome came to dominate the western Mediterranean. Syracuse, the Greek stronghold on Sicily, also became a Roman possession.

Rome did not have it all her own way, however. The Carthaginian general Hannibal (247–183/2 BCE) led his army on an epic march from Spain to northern Italy, famously bringing

BELOW: The Battle of the Aegetes in 241 BCE was a decisive maritime victory for Rome over Carthage, granting dominance in Sicily and the central Mediterranean and ending the First Punic War.

a force of war elephants over the Alps. He then conducted a long campaign in Italy, which caused Rome's allies to waver in their loyalty and old enemies to resurge. After suffering heavy defeats against Hannibal's forces Rome appointed Quintus Fabius Maximus Verrucosus to command her army.

Lacking the capability to defeat Hannibal in a decisive battle, and unwilling to risk Rome's last field force in Italy, Fabius Maximus pursued a strategy of delaying and wearing down Hannibal's army while avoiding major engagements. Although this 'Fabian strategy' was effective, pressure mounted for a more dramatic result. This was in part due to the risk that allies might defect if they felt Rome could not win her war.

Replacing Fabius Maximus in command, a large Roman army offered battle at Cannae, in 216 BCE. The dense Roman infantry formations were outflanked and encircled, resulting in a tremendous massacre. This shocking defeat was enough to persuade some Roman allies to break away. Carthage sent additional troops to Italy, but ultimately could not field sufficient fighters to force a victory.

After this, the worst defeat in Roman history, reforms of the military were undertaken. In the shorter term, the return to a Fabian strategy staved off defeat long enough for Rome to recover. The fall of Capua, which had led the defection from Rome to Carthage, demonstrated once again that Rome could not be defied. Despite the arrival of Carthaginian reinforcements their Italian campaign ended in defeat, after which Roman forces landed in North Africa. A decisive victory at Zama in 202 BCE broke Carthaginian resistance.

The Second Punic War ended with Carthage greatly diminished, but many considered she was a permanent threat to Rome. Marcus Porcius Cato (Cato the Elder; 234–149 BCE), holder of the post of censor, made his views clear by ending every speech with the declaration 'Delenda est Carthago' – Carthage must be destroyed.

The Third Punic War, of 149–146 BCE, was unnecessary in strategic terms, because Carthage was of little threat to Rome. However, she was still rich from trade. Urged by those who foresaw a new conflict with a resurgent Carthage – as well

MARCUS PORCIUS CATO MADE HIS VIEWS CLEAR – *DELENDA EST CARTHAGO* ('CARTHAGE MUST BE DESTROYED').

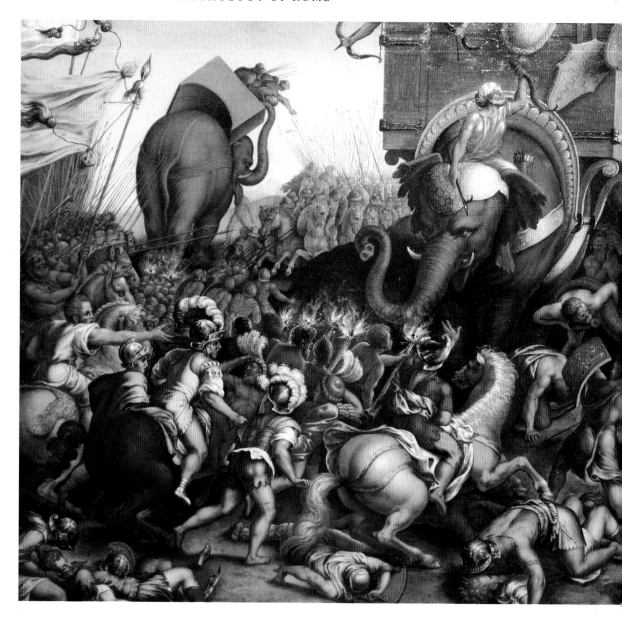

ABOVE: **This dramatic, if inaccurate, rendering of the Battle of Zama depicts the decisive defeat of Carthage in the Second Punic War.**

as those who merely wanted to plunder her riches – Roman officials found a pretext for war and launched a campaign, which was initially unsuccessful. Ultimately, however, Carthage was overwhelmed and her population sold into slavery.

The destruction of Carthage has passed into popular culture, though some of the details are distorted. The city was indeed brought to ruin, but the claim her fields were sown with salt seems unlikely. The amount of salt required to make a region infertile would be fabulously expensive, and in any case the

region soon became one of Rome's most important grain suppliers.

Other conflicts arose during this period. Conflict with Macedonia began in 215 BCE, when King Philip V attempted to exploit Rome's preoccupation with Carthage. The first Roman–Macedonian war ended in 205 BCE with a treaty unfavourable to Rome. Subsequent conflicts ran from 200 to 196 BCE and 171 to 168 BCE. These Second and Third Macedonian Wars were notable for the defeat of Macedonian phalanxes by more flexible Roman formations. The fourth and last Macedonian war was a short affair in 149–148 BCE, in which an attempt to reunify Macedonia as an autonomous state was quickly put down.

Evolution of the Roman army

The Roman army evolved throughout the city's long history. Beginning as an ad-hoc tribal force it developed into a heavy infantry-based form using phalanx formations. By the time of the Samnite Wars these had evolved into a more flexible organization, breaking the rigid phalanx up into maniples that deployed with gaps between them. This was the *quincunx* or 'checkerboard' formation.

The infantry of a legion formed up with the *hastati* in front. These were the youngest men, with the *principes* – more experienced men typically in their late 20s to 30s – forming a second line. If both were defeated, the veteran *triarii* could be relied on to cover a retreat or salvage a desperate situation. 'To fall back upon the *triarii*' was a Roman figure of speech referring

THE INFANTRY OF A LEGION FORMED UP WITH THE *HASTATI* IN FRONT.

to desperate measures. The poorest citizens, who could not afford the equipment needed to serve among the heavy infantry, fought as velites, or skirmishers.

The manipular legion was an effective fighting force, but the challenges faced by Rome were such that evolution was constant. Armour and equipment changed over time as a result of the threats a Roman soldier might encounter. Some equipment was adopted from allies and opponents. Among these was the gladius Hispaniensis, or 'Spanish sword', which impressed the Romans when they encountered it in the hands of Celtiberians. Well suited to close-order infantry combat, the gladius Hispaniensis has become the symbol of Roman soldiery even though other swords were used before and after it.

The Roman legion as most people imagine it came to be purely of necessity. The civic duty of men to serve in Rome's wars took artisans, traders and landowners out of the economic picture for an increasingly long time, adversely affecting the prosperity of the republic. The manpower shortage became a crisis in 110 BCE, while Rome was at war with King Jugurtha of Numidia. The problem was solved by Gaius Marius, who drastically reformed the Roman army.

BELOW: **A Roman legion of 206 BCE, with neat blocks of infantry capable of mutual support or independent manoeuvring.**

Previously, the poorest citizens had been exempt from military service because they could not outfit themselves. Under the new system they were paid and provided with equipment from state funds, establishing the army as a means by which the poor could better themselves. At the same time the state gained access to the largest segment of the population as potential recruits. Efficiency was improved by making the troops carry their own equipment, reducing the reliance on pack animals, and by standardizing arms and equipment. This was the emergence of the 'classic' Roman legion and its supporting practices. The settling of veterans in the provinces not only improved their loyalty and security, but also contributed to the Romanization of Europe.

Where the legions went, they took their gods. Garrisons built shrines, while settled veterans introduced worship of Roman gods to the local population. The spread of Roman religion was accompanied by the adoption of local gods as aspects of Roman deities, or sometimes in their own right. At the same time, Rome was a major factor in limiting the spread of Christianity once it developed. This was partly for religious reasons and partly to prevent the new belief from becoming a rallying point for dissent.

Transition to empire

Although determinedly hanging on to its republican traditions, Rome was an empire in all but name even before the rise of Gaius Julius Caesar (100–44 BCE). He trod the usual Roman path of lavish spending to buy political support, funded by his provincial governorship. Indeed, his famous campaign in Gaul was engineered to enrich himself and increase his reputation. By mistreating the Gallic tribes in his provinces, Caesar provoked a conflict and was given command of an army. After achieving his objectives he engaged in deliberate 'mission creep', finding new targets or crises that required his attention. Some of his great deeds, such as bridging the Rhine, were simply showboating.

Internal conflict was common among the powerful men of Rome, and Caesar's ascendance alarmed his opponents. He was summoned to the capital, but could not legally take his army into Roman territory. Faced with the choice of going unprotected to Rome, which was controlled by his enemies, or committing treason by bringing his army, Caesar chose to cross the Rubicon with his forces and trigger a civil war.

ABOVE: **Gaius Marius paved the way for later conquests by pushing through radical reforms of the Roman military system during the Jugurthine War.**

After a bitter conflict Caesar was master of the Roman world, at least until his assassination in 44 BCE. Although he was not explicitly the ruler of an empire, his name has become associated with absolute power. The German 'Kaiser' and Russian 'Tsar' are derived from Caesar's family name, and the latter has come to have new connotations in the modern world. A government minister placed in charge of an important field of endeavour may be referred to as a 'tsar', which – perhaps due to the gravitas associated with such titles – seems to imply greater capabilities than a typical government title.

The death of Julius Caesar saw a new phase in the internal political conflicts of the Roman world, from which his adopted son – originally named Gaius Octavius but better known as Augustus Caesar (63 BCE–14 CE) – emerged the dominant power. Augustus gradually pacified the Roman world, ushering in the 'Pax Romana'. This was a period of relative peace, which allowed the increased Romanization of Europe and the Mediterranean world. Although Rome was initially opposed to the spread of Christianity, the Pax Romana and the relative ease of movement it permitted were instrumental in allowing the new religion to take hold.

Augustus Caesar declared himself emperor in 31 BCE. The empire continued to expand and to consolidate its hold on the

BELOW: **Many of Julius Caesar's accomplishments, such as bridging the Rhine, and were geared towards enhancing his political career rather than serving any strategic need.**

areas it already controlled, but
its great size made internal
divisions inevitable and
stretched its forces very thin.
Despite a sophisticated system
of using auxiliary troops from
one region to garrison others,
making rebellions less likely,
the Pax Romana was never
a complete peace internally
and the borders were always
troubled.

Christianity and the empire

The appearance of what
seemed to be an obscure
Hebrew sect in the Middle East

ABOVE: **The deposition
of Emperor Flavius
Romulus Augustus
by Flavius Odoacer in
476AD was effectively
the end of the Western
Roman Empire.**

was of little consequence to the Roman empire. It was largely
irrelevant to the Jewish revolts of 66 CE and 135 CE, though
Roman interference in Jewish religious practices was a factor
in both. This reflects a problem encountered by conquerors
throughout history – people may accept a change of rulership but
interference with their gods will trigger determined resistance.

Christianity continued to spread throughout the Roman
world despite resistance and at times savage persecution. The
Roman religion remained ascendant, however, until at least
313 CE. By this time the Roman world was divided into eastern
and western segments, which were different in character. By
the Edict of Milan, both halves of the empire were granted
freedom to worship whatever gods a citizen pleased. Previous to
this, tolerance and persecution had alternated according to the
current leadership.

The old Roman religion was displaced relatively quickly
after this, and by 391 CE Christianity was the official religion
of the empire. Worship of the old gods was outlawed, though
it may have continued in some areas. By this time the empire
was under severe pressure, with populations who had previously

been Roman in character beginning to find their own identity. The overthrow of the last Roman emperor in 47 CE is generally considered to be the end of the empire, though the eastern half endured. This became the Byzantine empire and had little to do with the old religion.

Roman mythology

The commonly accepted version of Roman mythology is associated with the republic and early empire, but has links going back to ancient Greece and the proto-Indo-European religion. Similarities between the Roman and Greek deities are not coincidental; Greek culture was extremely influential and in many cases mythology was adopted wholesale. This caused major changes to the Roman gods of the time, and may have obliterated earlier myths.

Population movement and trade caused further cultural mingling, and brought influences from elsewhere. Greece had links with India, causing cultural elements and ideas to percolate throughout the Mediterranean world. Rome herself had interactions with Persia and Egypt, as well as the Gauls and the people of eastern North Africa. All of these elements influenced Roman mythology as we today perceive it.

Roman mythology was not static. It changed and developed over time, and was amended for political purposes or influenced

BELOW: **Like many Greek goddesses, Gaia – depicted here in mosaic form – had a Roman equivalent. She was generally known as Terra Mater, but the Greek name was also used.**

by changing cultural values. Any given myth or story must be presented as a snapshot of what was believed in a particular place at a particular time. There is no single, definitive version to be found anywhere, though there are commonly accepted variants based on the works of influential writers. The Roman republic and empire are responsible for spreading these beliefs sufficiently widely that they are part of European culture hundreds of years later, and ultimately the history of Rome itself fades into myth the further back we look.

Cosmology and the beginnings of the universe

The ancient Romans had a pragmatic view of religion, using it like any other tool. Worship was directed towards gods who could provide assistance or whose wrath was best averted. Thus the early origins of the universe and the primal gods who existed there were of relatively little interest to the average Roman. However, they sought an explanation for the existence of the earth, sea and sky, and for the stars and planets they could see above them.

The Roman creation story has much in common with that of the ancient Greeks, as described in the epic poem Theogony. This was created by the Greek writer Hesiod around 700 BCE, and appears to have been adopted wholesale by the early Romans. Later writers, notably Publius Ovidius Naso – better known as Ovid (43 BCE–17 CE) – expanded on the mythology they had inherited. Of course, Ovid was writing seven centuries after Hesiod, so his perception of the myths was filtered through a different social and cultural environment.

According to Hesiod, the universe began as formless matter containing the potential for everything. This is referred to as Chaos and is considered to be a primal god. Chaos gave birth to five offspring. They were Nyx, Gaia, Tartarus, Erebus and Eros in the original Greek version. In the Romanized variant of Hesiod's account, the goddess Tellus (Gaia) personified the earth and Tartarus – whose name remains unchanged – the underworld. Nox (Nyx) was the goddess of Night, and Scotos (Erebus) represented darkness. The fifth child of Chaos was named Cupid

ABOVE: The Greek goddess Nyx, depicted here, is known as Nox in Roman mythology. Her stories and role are virtually unchanged.

Nox

Nox is both obscure and powerful. In some versions of the creation story she is even older than Chaos, a dark emptiness that filled the universe before Chaos brought potentiality. Parallels to the modern Big Bang Theory are obvious – Nox is the empty universe and Chaos is the single point containing all the energy and matter that will ever exist. Nox is sometimes credited with being the mother of Scotos, in partnership with Chaos, as well as having offspring with him. According to some accounts, Nox is the only being feared by Jupiter, because she is so all-encompassing as to be beyond even his power.

RIGHT: The Dutch artist Hendrick Goltzius produced a series of plates depicting deities. This is Aether, god of the upper air.

in the Romanized version, personifying love or desire, but should not be confused with the Cupids who are the children of Venus and Mars.

Tellus gave birth to Caelus, who represented the heavens and became her husband. This represented a union of earth and sky, which resulted in the birth of various magical creatures. More significantly for the cosmos, their children Saturn and Ops would become the parents of several major Roman gods. Nox and Scotos produced Aether, god of the upper air, and Dies – the personification of day. These primordial deities played little part in Roman religion other than to explain the formation and nature of the world and to provide an explanation of where the current set of gods came from.

The separation of chaos caused the world to settle into a form that could be inhabited by mortals. The sky and the upper air, the earth and the underworld all became established, and the primal gods personified and governed the parts of the world. The natural order was established with night and day, but elements of the present world may have still been missing. It is not clear whether the sun and moon existed before their respective deities came into existence, nor whether the year had seasons before the actions of the gods caused them to come into being.

The Orphic myths

Some of the alternative versions of Roman myths come from Orphic tradition. This was based on teachings supposedly left behind by the legendary Greek musician Orpheus. Orpheus himself is a mythological figure of semi-divine parentage whose music could cause boulders and trees to dance.

Whatever the origins of these myths, they formed part of a 'mystery cult' of Orphism that was practised across the Greek and Roman world. As with all mystery religions, Orphism revealed its secrets only to those who were initiated. It is likely that the Orphic version of the popular Roman and Greek myths would have been part of this body of knowledge, revealed perhaps as 'secret truths the Priests of Jupiter don't want you to know!'

The Orphic myths state that Chaos was the product of other primordial forces. These were Time, personified by the primal god Chronus, and Necessity, referred to as Adrasteia or Ananke depending on the source. These myths state that other primordial beings named Scotos and Aether were born along with Chaos, but do not appear to consider them deities as such.

In the Orphic tradition, the first deity was Phanes, also known as Protogonus, who is described as the child of Chronus and Aether. Phanes was both male and female, and gave birth to Nox, whom they made ruler of the universe. In time Nox passed on the mantle of rulership to her son Caelus, whom she warned would be overthrown by his children. This warning was in vain; Caelus was castrated and brought down by his son Saturn. He in turn was deposed by his son Jupiter, enabling the classical Roman gods to take control of the universe.

BELOW: The Orphic myths are based upon secrets supposedly left behind by the great musician and adventurer Orpheus, who was taught to play by Apollo himself.

2

THE PRIMARY DEITIES

The 12 primary Roman deities are known as the *Dii Consentes*, forming a council headed by Jupiter. These 12 deities would be at the centre of a Roman citizen's religious life, with other gods worshipped whenever it seemed appropriate. Which deity was of the greatest importance to a given citizen depended on their circumstances and might change frequently.

More is known about the mythology and religion of Rome than most other ancient civilizations as a result of surviving writings. From them, it is clear that the Roman state derived its legitimacy and preserved its well-being by maintaining a good relationship with the gods. Indeed, Roman religion was largely concerned with regulating the interplay between gods and mortals by the correct performance of appropriate rituals and avoiding behaviour that might anger the gods. Virgil's *Aeneid* is an example of the

OPPOSITE: **The painting 'Feast of the Gods' was first created by Bellini then modified by his pupil, Titian. It depicts a scene from Ovid's writings.**

archetypical Roman hero – Aeneas is above all dutiful in carrying out the commands of the gods despite the great personal cost.

The relationship, or peace, between mortals and deities is known as Pax Deorum. This was sufficiently important that a set of religious laws – jus divinum – was drawn up to ensure the correct observances were made. The head of state in early Rome was a religious as well as a political and military leader, and later the role of priest-king became a lifetime office, while secular authority was vested in a pair of elected consuls who served for only one year.

ABOVE: Aeneas is depicted rescuing his father from the burning remains of Troy before setting out on an epic voyage that would end in Italy.

Early Roman religion was clearly heavily influenced by Greek mythology, to the point where gods seem to have been co-opted wholesale along with their myths and stories. Those myths that are of Roman origin tend to deal with matters such as the founding of the city – and even then they connect back to the Greek myths. There is also a tendency to identify foreign gods as aspects of their own. For example, a tribe of Gauls is described in Roman writings about them as worshipping Mercury, which is highly unlikely. They had gods of their own, which were correlated with Roman deities for a variety of reasons.

It is possible that the Roman historians recording what they knew about people beyond the borders were simply mistaken, or were attempting to simplify the situation rather than explain the details of a complex foreign religion. It was also convenient for the people along the borders to have the same gods. This avoided any affront to the Roman gods if they acknowledged those of another culture and made subjugation much easier. By quietly

THE ARCHAIC AND CAPITOLINE TRIADS

Triads of gods and goddesses were an institution inherited from the Etruscans, who built three-chambered temples to the associated deities. Some sources state that the original (Archaic) triad of gods worshipped in Rome were Jupiter, Mars and Quirinus. The latter may have been of Sabine origin, but is often said to be the deified form of the founder Romulus.

If the Archaic Triad existed at all, it was replaced by the Capitoline Triad (named after the Capitoline Hill on which they were worshipped). These, the most important of all Roman gods, were Jupiter, Juno and Minerva. It is notable that the war god Mars is displaced by Minerva, a goddess associated with strategic warfare. It may be that whereas early Rome needed noisy heroes, her later ascendency was built on meticulous planning and sophisticated organization, and the choice of war god reflected this change.

BELOW: **The Capitoline Triad of Jupiter, Juno and Minerva can be taken to represent the leaders, the people and the warriors of Rome, all of whom contributed to her greatness.**

redefining the local gods as Roman ones, the conquerors avoided having to impose an external religion, with all of the difficulties that inevitably entails.

Religion in ancient Rome

Roman mythology and religion evolved over time. Early influences came from the nearby powers such as the Sabines and the Etruscan city-states, with an increase in Greek influence until Roman mythology and religious practice closely resembled those of Greece. Indeed, in the parts of Italy that had been Greek colonies it was not uncommon for Greek and Roman names to be used interchangeably.

Early Rome established itself by welcoming new citizens from all around the Mediterranean world, and they brought their gods and stories with them. Some were forgotten or received little prominence, but others became part of a more-or-less unified mythology that belonged to Rome, but whose elements originated elsewhere. By the mid-sixth century BCE most of the Roman gods had evolved into the forms we know today, though some were added to the pantheon much later.

As Rome itself grew in wealth and stature, temples were constructed in prominent locations to honour the primary gods, and rituals became standardized. This was extremely important, and an incorrectly performed ritual might not please the deity it was directed to. Failure to honour a relevant god or being at the right time could also bring about misfortune. This was in essence breach of contract, and if mortals failed in their obligations the gods were not obliged to bless their activities.

Some rituals took place on set days and were necessary to maintain the favour of the gods, whereas others were triggered by circumstances. Celebrating a Triumph was not just about honouring the deeds of a general; it also gave due respect to Jupiter as the patron of an ascendant Rome and of powerful Roman citizens. Other rituals were daily and private matters, some conducted regularly and others when one wanted to ask for something specific from the gods. This was known as the votum and was essentially a private contract to give worship in return for assistance.

IN THE PARTS OF ITALY THAT HAD BEEN GREEK COLONIES IT WAS NOT UNCOMMON FOR GREEK AND ROMAN NAMES TO BE USED INTERCHANGEABLY.

ABOVE: Dating from 498 BCE, though rebuilt later, the Temple of Saturn is the oldest religious structure in Rome.

Rome's early kings were religious leaders for the whole state, and later a class of senior priests led the worship of the major gods or officiated over specific festivals. In addition to formal ceremonies, auguries were extremely important to all activities. Before any endeavour the omens would be read and plans changed until a promising set of omens presented itself. Those who failed to conduct an augury, or who acted when the omens were poor, generally met with disaster.

Religion played an important part within organizations such as the legions, and also within the family. The male head of a household was also its religious leader, offering worship to the primary deities as well as the ancestors and household gods of the family. The exact rituals performed varied from family to family, but it was held that the Roman state as a whole depended on families carrying out these domestic duties.

The family and household gods pre-dated the pantheon we know today, and some of the gods grew out of these traditions. Notable among these is Janus, god of doorways, and the goddess Vesta who became a member of the *Dii Consentes*. Other gods remained minor but were still revered, with a family shrine or statues kept in the home and small domestic rituals performed

VESTA

VESTAE   SACRVM
C. PVPIVS FIRMINVS ET
MVDASENA   TROPHIME

ABOVE: Vesta was worshipped as a household goddess, and on a rather more grand scale as a major deity of the Roman state.

in their name. Roman citizens were careful to avoid angering even the small gods because serious consequences might befall them if an observance was missed or incorrectly performed. There were even segments of rituals devoted essentially to 'any god not mentioned here who feels they should have been' or 'gods we do not know but respect all the same'.

Rome even waged a form of religious warfare, adopting the worship of gods associated with their enemies in order to draw away their favour. It is possible that the worship of Venus began this way. Seeking an advantage over the Carthaginians, the Romans effectively stole their goddess. This was an aspect of Venus associated with the city of Eryx in Sicily. Capturing the likeness of Venus from the city and setting up a magnificent temple, the Romans caused Venus to become one of their deities and removed her support from the Carthaginian cause.

The practice of honouring emperors as living gods was initially implemented alongside the traditional worship of the pantheon, but over time became more important. Religion also changed considerably as a result of outside influences. Examples include the rise of Mithraism and the adoption of Christianity by an increasingly large segment of the Roman population. The religion of the later empire bore little resemblance to that of early Rome or the republican era.

The primal gods

The greatest of the Roman gods was Jupiter, but he was not the original ruler of the universe. This was Caelus, who personified

PRIESTS AND OTHER RELIGIOUS PROFESSIONALS

Although the people of ancient Rome worshipped many gods, some priests were devoted exclusively to one and were known collectively as flamines. Each individual flamen, assisted by his wife, offered daily sacrifices to their associated deity and observed a rigidly specified lifestyle. Once the practice of deifying emperors began, additional flamines were appointed to worship them. Those assigned to distant provinces typically also had a political role.

The supreme religious figure in Rome's earliest days was also its ruler, but these offices were separated and the position of Rex Sacrorum created. This king-of-all-things-sacred answered to the pontifex maximus, who also held authority over the flamen and the pontifices. The latter advised the pontifex maximus on matters of religious law, and later formed part of the College of Pontifices.

As the College of Pontifices expanded it came to include the flamines and the Rex Sacrorum along with the Vestal Virgins, who tended the temple of Vesta. Originally selected from patrician families, this office was eventually opened to plebians. Service in the temple began at a young age and was governed by strict rules. Vestal Virgins could retire after 30 years of service, at which point their vow of chastity no longer applied.

Among the other full-time religious figures of ancient Rome were professional augurs, who were widely employed by those who might need to determine the omens before an action. This might be a political gambit, planting of crops or a business deal. Augurs were consulted in legal cases, sometimes leading to decisions that might otherwise seem rather strange.

BELOW: **The flamines were forbidden to go out in pubic unless they were wearing the Apex, a sacred cap topped with a piece of olive wood.**

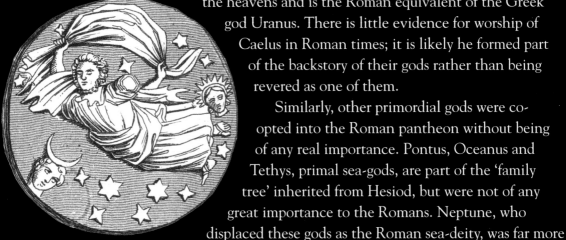

the heavens and is the Roman equivalent of the Greek god Uranus. There is little evidence for worship of Caelus in Roman times; it is likely he formed part of the backstory of their gods rather than being revered as one of them.

Similarly, other primordial gods were co-opted into the Roman pantheon without being of any real importance. Pontus, Oceanus and Tethys, primal sea-gods, are part of the 'family tree' inherited from Hesiod, but were not of any great importance to the Romans. Neptune, who displaced these gods as the Roman sea-deity, was far more prominent. This reflects a pragmatic worship of the 'gods of now' rather than their progenitors and predecessors, who were not in a position to provide assistance to mortals.

Sources vary on the nature and relationships of the primal gods, and in many cases the earliest myths appear to be translations or adaptations of the ancient Greek versions. In this tradition, the universe sprang from a cosmic egg, dividing into atoms that formed layers. The highest was the 'bright air' or aether, while the heaviest sank to become the oceans. The earth took its place in between.

The parts of the early cosmos were personified by deities, with Caelus personifying the bright heavens. Caelus was married to Tellus (or Terra), personification of the Earth and equivalent to Gaia in Greek mythology. Caelus was a cruel husband, and Tellus plotted against him with her children. Among them was Saturn, and to him Tellus gave a magical scythe she had fashioned. Most accounts refer to it as being made of flint, which is often ascribed powers against the supernatural or paranormal. With this weapon Saturn castrated his father and overthrew him. In addition to making Saturn the pre-eminent god, this deed had other consequences. The blood of Caelus fell on the sea, causing the goddess Venus to spring into being, and on the land, where it spawned the Furies.

The usurpation of power by Saturn was a major event for the entire cosmos. Previously, a state of chaos had existed in which boundless possibilities were present. Saturn's ascendance was

ABOVE: Caelus was the original ruler of the heavens but was eclipsed by Saturn who was in turn overthrown by Jupiter. Unlike Caelus, Saturn remained an important god in the Roman pantheon.

the beginning of cosmic regulation, with the heavens moving in an orderly fashion dictated by time. This was a universe where mortals could exist, whereas previously the chaos was incomprehensible. Only gods could live there.

Saturn married his sister, Ops, who was an earth goddess possibly of Sabine origin. He is also associated with the goddess Lua, though some sources suggest Lua is an aspect or alternative name for Ops. This union of a sky god and an earth goddess produced six children: Jupiter, Juno, Neptune, Pluto, Ceres and Vesta. In an attempt to avoid being displaced by his own

LEFT: A relief dating from 13 BCE, depicting Romulus and Remus in the care of Tellus.

children, as he had done to Caelus, Saturn ate most of them as they were born.

Last born was Jupiter, whose mother decided to save him by substituting a rock for the baby. In some versions of the story this caused Saturn to vomit up the rest of his children. Saturn's fears were then realized when his children overthrew him, setting up Jupiter as the ruler of the cosmos. In an alternative version the last of the children, Jupiter, was hidden until he came into his power, then used the same scythe with which Saturn had castrated Caelus to overpower his father and rescue his siblings. In some versions of the tale Saturn was dismembered and sent to the underworld, but the popular Roman variant had him escape and go into hiding. The place he chose became known as Latium, where Saturn instigated a golden age of plenty.

Saturn's association with time was extremely important to the Roman people, because prosperity depended on sowing and harvesting at the right times. By placing the seasons in their correct order Saturn ensured mortals could thrive. His temple in Rome at times served as a treasury as well as a place of worship, and

BELOW: The image of Saturn devouring his children has inspired many art pieces. This one, by Lazar Wideman, dates from 1740.

THE SIGNIFICANCE OF MYTHS

Greek mythology includes the Titanomachy, a tremendous struggle between the gods and their predecessors, known as Titans, for control of the universe. Given the similarities between the Roman and Greek gods and their myths, this event must have taken place – in some form – within Roman mythology. However, it does not have the prominence given to it by the Greeks, even though it is a tremendous story of enormous importance to the whole universe.

This is perhaps due to the differing nature of Greek and Roman mythology. To a great extent Roman religion was concerned with relationships among the deities and between gods and mortals, with the myths and stories serving to illustrate and explain them. Greek mythology seems to be more concerned with the stories; the relationships that drive them are necessary but not the focus. Greek and Roman mythology might be considered two different views of the same mythic events. The Greeks were excited by what happened, whereas the Romans were careful to note its significance.

ABOVE: Although Roman mythology contained epic events such as the defeat of the Titans, worshippers were more concerned with their current relationship than with backstory.

he is associated with the festival of Saturnalia. This was held around the winter solstice and was characterized by indulgence, forgiveness and gift-giving. Although known by a different name, the spirit of this festival has lived on into the modern world.

Jupiter

Jupiter, also known as Jove, is the leader – and in some cases the father – of the Roman gods. His name may derive from an Indo-European word meaning Father of the Light. Over time this evolved to Iuppiter, or Deiu-Pater, and hence to its modern form. Jupiter is associated with stormy skies, lightning and thunder, and was worshipped on hilltops. The temple of Jupiter Optimus Maximus, atop the Capitoline Hill in Rome, was the greatest of the city's temples and the final destination of a military commander returning in triumph to the city.

Jupiter had multiple aspects that might receive worship depending on the needs of the worshipper. Iuppiter Tonans was associated with thunder and lightning, and with the rain needed by farmers. In this aspect, Jupiter is said to have taught the early Romans how to dodge lightning – a metaphor perhaps for his protection of the city and her people. Iuppiter Optimus Maximus was acknowledged as the greatest of all the gods and necessary to the investiture of a king. Before the republic was founded, Roman kings were given imperium – the authority to command others – in a ceremony dedicated to Jupiter. As previously noted, the early history of Rome is as much myth as it is historical record. According to a common version of the founding-story, the worship of Jupiter began with a pact between Numa Pompilius, successor to Romulus as king of Rome, and the god himself. The pact was facilitated by Faunas and Picus, minor deities who were persuaded to summon Jupiter.

Jupiter agreed to become the patron of Rome and her protector in return for sacrifices and worship, which was to be

ABOVE: **Association with Jupiter lent legitimacy to Roman leaders and generals, setting them above ordinary mortals.**

Triumph

A Triumph was a celebration of a great victory, and as such had both civic and religious elements. It consisted of a procession from the Triumphal Gate to the temple of Jupiter on the Capitoline Hill. There, a great sacrifice of animals and prisoners of war was undertaken in honour of Jupiter and the triumphant general.

The victorious commander personified Jupiter during his Triumph, dressing in a purple toga and holding Jupiter's sceptre. His face was coloured red to signify his divine link. Strict rules dictated what deeds were required to qualify for a Triumph. Those who performed well but did not qualify might instead be rewarded with a lesser ceremony called an ovatio.

BELOW: **A Triumph was an extremely lavish affair which ensured Jupiter received proper credit for his role in the general's great victory.**

conducted in the manner he prescribed. He gifted the city with a perfectly round shield referred to as the ancile, and, along with 11 near-perfect copies made in Rome, this became a symbol of the relationship between Jupiter and Rome. This relationship evolved over time. In the days of the republic, Jupiter was the main deity and the protector of Rome, but once the emperors began to be worshipped as gods, they displaced Jupiter and his worship declined. The adoption of Christianity resulted in the abolition of Jupiter worship.

Jupiter's ascension to supreme status ushered in a new order in the universe. His brother Pluto was given command over the underworld, and Neptune dominion over the oceans. Jupiter himself ruled the air, while the earth was of common interest to all of them. He married his sister Juno and with her had Vulcanus (god of fire) and Mars (god of war). Jupiter was not by any means a faithful husband, however, which caused a certain amount of marital friction.

In some myths Jupiter is credited with fathering Venus, though other tales have her originating as a result of the castration of Caelus. Jupiter was the parent of Minerva by unusual means, and more conventionally of Mercury, Apollo and Diana, among others. He was also partial to mortal women, fathering with them the hero Hercules and the god Bacchus.

Juno

Juno was the sister of Jupiter, daughter of Saturn and Ops. As the wife of Jupiter she was responsible for governing the lives of women, but her many aspects covered a much wider range of roles. Juno was worshipped as a queen and a bringer of timely warnings, a saviour of the needy and a bringer of light and enlightenment. In her role as mother and protector of women, Juno controlled the menstrual cycle and childbirth.

Despite this generally domestic identity, Juno had a warlike aspect. This may have reflected an expansion of her role from protector of women to defender of all people within the Roman state. Similarly, her role as the governor of married life matched her position as queen of the gods – her husband was their king, after all. Juno was also associated with cycles, as well as female fertility, the seasons and the phases of

BELOW: Whilst primarily a supportive deity, Juno was also a warrior who would protect the people of Rome when the need arose.

the moon. In the latter capacity she is sometimes described as a moon-goddess, but she was not a personification of the moon. Instead, she governed its behaviour as part of her divine remit.

Worship of Juno probably began with the Etruscans, and was certainly common in the early days of Rome as a city. Although she was not part of the Archaic Triad, Juno appears to have replaced Quirinus by the time the Capitoline Triad became pre-eminent. If Minerva is assumed to replace Mars as the war god of the trio, then Juno takes the place of Quirinus. There are numerous explanations for this, not least the tidy relationship of husband, wife and daughter as leader, facilitator and warrior. It may also be that Quirinus, as possibly the deified form of the founder Romulus, was less important at that time than Juno, who was definitely wife and mother to gods.

The relationship between Juno and her husband was often strained, largely due to Jupiter's infidelity. Juno rightly suspected her husband of cheating, and tried to thwart him whenever she

ABOVE: **Jupiter's unsuccessful attempt to deceive his wife resulted in the murder of the faithful Argus, who surely deserved better.**

could. Failing that, she would punish Jupiter's lovers. One such was Io, a priestess of Jupiter. To protect Io (and possibly himself) from Juno's wrath Jupiter turned Io into a heifer and tried to sell his wife a story about it being a gift for her.

Juno was not convinced, and sent a creature named Argus to watch the heifer with his hundred eyes. This was inconvenient for Jupiter and Io alike, so Jupiter enlisted the help of Mercury. His solution was rather direct; he lulled Argus to sleep and killed him. As usual in such tales, the desires of the gods outweighed the life of an innocent who happened to be caught in the middle of their affairs. Juno honoured Argus by placing his eyes on the tail of the peacock and pursued Io, who was still in the form of a heifer. Transforming herself into a gadfly, Juno bit and tormented Io, who wandered the world seeking escape. Eventually Juno decided Io had suffered enough and transformed her back into a woman.

JUNO HONOURED ARGUS BY PLACING HIS EYES ON THE TAIL OF THE PEACOCK AND PURSUED IO, WHO WAS STILL IN THE FORM OF A HEIFER.

Neptune

One of the siblings of Jupiter and Juno, Neptune was saved from his father's belly by Jupiter and subsequently became lord of the seas. He was originally worshipped as a god of fresh water, but had evolved into the primary ocean deity by 400 BCE. This may have resulted from increased interest in the seas as an avenue for trade and commerce; Rome did not become a maritime power until forced to do so by conflict with Carthage. It is notable that Neptune's primary festival is in July, when the rivers and wells might be drying up for lack of rainfall. This is a holdover from Neptune's days as the lord of fresh water, when citizens would offer worship in the hope Neptune would be generous.

Neptune was also associated with horses and horse racing, but his primary role was as lord of the sea and its storms. His importance grew as Rome developed into a maritime power, but he remained a god of specific functions rather

than becoming a leader. Propitiating Neptune was extremely important to sailors and those with dubious water supplies, but beyond this Neptune was of relatively minor importance.

Neptune's wife is sometimes said to be Salacia, goddess of saltwater, and in other sources is named as Amphitrite. She was originally a nymph, a minor supernatural being, and initially preferred to remain so. She fled from Neptune's advances and hid in the Atlantic Ocean, but was tracked down and persuaded to return by a dolphin sent by Neptune. The dolphin was well rewarded for his service, becoming the constellation Delphinus, and on her union with Neptune Salacia (or Amphitrite) gained in importance to become a goddess.

The Atlantic Ocean was known to the ancient Romans, though they had no idea of its extent or its far shores. Greek

BELOW: Neptune is typically depicted riding a chariot pulled by horses, which often have fish-like tails.

expeditions had passed through the Straits of Gibraltar and explored the northern seas, and their findings were known to the Romans. These expeditions followed the coasts, of course, so the wide expanse of the Atlantic was the most distant and mysterious sea known to the Romans. Even Neptune knew little about the ocean, and was unable to find Salacia without assistance.

Salacia and Neptune had four children: Benthesikyme, Rhodes, Triton and Proteus. Triton was a sea-god much like his father, and Proteus had knowledge of all things past, present and future. He was not forthcoming with information, however. He could change his shape and would use this ability to escape anyone who came to see him. Only those who caught him by surprise had any chance to speak with Proteus, and even then they had to bind him while he changed shape and fought to escape.

Neptune may have had little power on the land, but he was the one who shaped it into its present form. Striking the ground with his trident, he summoned a great rush of waters across the land and the seabed. In so doing he destroyed or submerged everything, with only two humans surviving. When he was done, Neptune instructed his son Triton to summon the waters back

BELOW: Upon marrying Neptune, Salacia became a goddess. She is depicted here riding her own chariot alongside that of Neptune.

by blowing on a conch shell. The river valleys and coastlines that emerged from this great flood are those we know today.

Pluto

Another sibling of Jupiter and Juno, Pluto was given lordship over the underworld and the dead. Although this consigned him to a rather dismal realm compared with the mighty oceans or the boundless skies, it did give Pluto great power. Not only could he influence the fortunes of mortals, but the world's wealth was also located in his realm – Pluto was the god of metals and gemstones, and revered as a bringer of wealth.

For the most part Pluto lived apart from the mortal world, and played only a small role in the affairs of mortals and gods. An

ABOVE: **Pluto's rather grim underworld realm also contained the riches of the Earth, though this seems to have brought him little joy.**

attempt by Venus to improve his life by finding him someone to love was probably well-meant but caused great suffering for gods and mortals. Like many actions of the gods, helping someone usually meant harming someone else. In this case, Venus sent her son Cupid to shoot love-arrows at Pluto, which resulted in him falling in love with the next woman he encountered.

The unfortunate victim of Pluto's desire was Proserpina, goddess of spring and daughter of Ceres. Pluto forced her into his chariot and raced back to his underground realm, leaving only a belt and a bow behind as clues to what had happened. Ceres, distraught, searched for her daughter but could find nothing more than these items, and Pluto denied all knowledge of the incident.

Ceres' grief at the loss of her daughter was so great that she ceased to fulfil her divine functions. Crops failed and animals starved, causing great suffering in the world of mortals. This

was of no little concern to the gods, because their relationship with mortals was a two-way street. If the rituals were performed but the gods did not respond with prosperity and good fortune, mortals might stop worshipping. Therefore, other gods joined the search, among them Mercury.

Mercury was able to move between worlds, and soon located Proserpina in the realm of Pluto. Jupiter was informed, and immediately demanded her release. Pluto agreed, on condition that if Proserpina had taken any food in the underworld she would have to stay. She had indeed eaten, but just a few pomegranate seeds, so in the end a bargain was struck. Proserpina would have to stay in the underworld for half the year, during which time her mother Ceres would grieve and the world would be barren. In the spring, Proserpina would come back to the surface world and her mother's joy would drive away the winter.

Thus for all his detachment from the world, Pluto – or arguably Venus by way of Pluto – unintentionally caused the seasons to come into being. This would affect all mortals for the rest of time. As for Proserpina, she is without a doubt the victim of the tale. Everyone else benefits – Pluto gets a wife for half the year and the world is not plunged into eternal winter – but Proserpina is trapped in a marriage she did not want and must spend half the year in the gloomy underworld.

Thus it is with the Roman gods – they are powerful but not necessarily benevolent. It is not clear whether Venus cared about the suffering she wrought upon Proserpina, and the other gods seem more concerned with restoring the fertility of the surface world than righting any wrongs.

Death and the underworld

Roman belief about what happened after death was in the main adopted from the Greeks, and there is evidence that beliefs may have varied according to time and place. Certainly, different funerary practices prevailed at times, though there is no sign of a clear and simple progression. Burial and cremation were both used, one becoming more popular than the other for a period before preferences changed again. Much of what we know about the Roman underworld comes from the *Aeneid*, which describes

OPPOSITE: An 18th century depiction of the Rape of Proserpina. The story is about powerful gods exercising their power with little regard for the suffering of lesser beings.

ABOVE: **A Renaissance depiction of Charon, the boatman who conveyed dead souls across the River Styx.**

the journey of Aeneas through its regions. The first three of these are crossed by all dead souls, until they reach the banks of the River Styx. Those who have not received a proper funeral are doomed to wait there forever. Souls who have been properly put to rest may cross, and will either enter the pleasant fields of Elysium or suffer the torments of Tartarus.

One reason for funeral rites was to ensure the departed soul was correctly sent on its way to the afterlife. This was important to the departed, of course, but also protected the living by ensuring the dead could get across the River Styx. If not, they might harass the living until properly put to rest. Further protection from problems associated with death was afforded by segregating burial grounds from inhabited areas. The boundary of a community was known as the pomerium and was both a physical and a metaphysical border, with no burials permitted within.

A mourning period of eight days was observed, during which the family of the departed withdrew from daily life. After this the departed soul was well on its way to the underworld and would not hang around causing problems for the living. The dead were still honoured, especially if they had done great deeds in their life or possessed considerable wealth.

The process was rather different for Roman emperors, who were deified after (and in some cases before) their deaths. The practice, known as apotheosis, began with Julius Caesar and became standard for succeeding emperors. Before this only one Roman mortal had been deified. This was Quirinus, who had previously been the mortal Romulus.

Ceres

Ceres was a sibling of Jupiter who protected the common people (plebians) and was the primary goddess of fertility and agriculture. With Liber and Libera, also agricultural deities, Ceres was a member of the Aventine Triad whose three-chambered temple stood on the Aventine Hill. Ceres was the subject of a number of festivals throughout the year, each connected with a phase of the growing and harvesting seasons.

Ceres was widely worshipped by the common people of Rome, as the bringer of bountiful food. Indeed, the word 'cereal' derives from her name. She was also the personal adviser and protector of the Tribune of the Plebians, who represented the ordinary folk who might otherwise be subject to the whims of the noble (patrician) class. This relationship made harming the Tribune of the Plebians a crime against the gods, granting a level of protection that might be quite necessary when going against the interests of the nobility.

Despite being at the centre of one of the most important Roman myths – the abduction of Proserpina – Ceres is not credited with great deeds or leadership of grand endeavours because she is a supportive deity rather than a great

BELOW: Despite her importance as a provider and protector, Ceres was very much a supportive goddess rather than an assertive figure.

force in the cosmos. She is often depicted carrying a torch in reference to her search for her daughter, Proserpina.

Vesta

Vesta was the unassuming goddess of hearth and home. She is sometimes referred to as Mater (mother) but remained virginal throughout her existence. Her priestesses were also required to be celibate, and were known as Vestales, or Vestal Virgins. As a supportive goddess, Vesta played a minor role in the mythology of Rome but was immensely important to the common people, who worshipped her. These included folk of all social levels and

RIGHT: **The Vestal Virgins tended the temple of Vesta, ensuring its eternal flame never went out.**

occupations, but Vesta was particularly associated with millers and bakers.

Among the symbols associated with Vesta is the donkey, which has connotations of milling using animal power, but also features in a tale of how Vesta was saved from rape. She attended a party hosted by Cybele, at which everyone except her over-indulged. Among the inebriated guests was Silenus, who tutored Bacchus and shared his passion for wine. Silenus used a donkey for transport but was too drunk to secure it properly.

ABOVE: Latona, a former wife of Jupiter, was hounded by a vengeful Juno. She gave birth to Apollo and Diana under difficult circumstances.

Vesta withdrew from the party and rather innocently sought a place to sleep. Careless of her safety, she was spotted by a lustful nature deity named Priapus. Priapus resolved to rape the sleeping Vesta but was disturbed by the wandering donkey, whose braying alerted everyone nearby. Priapus was thrown out of the party and forbidden to attend any others, and Vesta remained a virgin.

Vesta was one of the earliest deities worshipped in Rome, and her festival continued even after the adoption of Christianity as the state religion. This made Vesta the last non-Christian god in Rome. Her temple in the Forum housed the 'eternal flame', which it was said would burn for as long as Rome endured.

Apollo

Although most of the Roman gods have Greek counterparts, they are known by different names. Apollo, on the other hand, has the same identity in both pantheons. The personification of an orderly and law-abiding society, Apollo was also a musician and patron of both medicine and disease. He was the patron of oracles, dispensed wisdom to prophets and bestowed enlightenment on those who worshipped him.

Worship of Apollo was adopted from the Greeks, probably around 433 BCE. This was a pragmatic move on the part of the

Romans, who needed protection from a plague. The connection of Apollo with medicine might offer salvation, and since Apollo was also the causer of plagues propitiating him might be wise. Once begun, worship continued and became more widespread during the first years of the Roman empire. Augustus, first emperor of Rome, considered Apollo to be his patron and benefactor and built a new temple on the Palatine Hill.

Apollo's myths were also adopted wholesale from the Greeks, albeit with some changes to names. His mother was Latona, a Titan who was married to Jupiter. While she was pregnant, Latona and Jupiter separated. Jupiter's new wife Juno was jealous, and sent a monster named Python to harass her predecessor. Even unborn, Apollo showed his great wisdom by guiding his mother to safety.

Latona found sanctuary on the island of Delos, but Juno was not yet finished with her. She held the goddess of midwifery, Lucina, captive while Latona struggled to give birth. She had been pregnant with twins, of whom the first to be born was Diana. Diana came into the world fully adult and in possession of her powers, and was able to help her mother in birthing Apollo.

Apollo was not quite so precocious as Diana, but grew to adulthood in a matter of days. Given weapons by Vulcanus, the god of fire, Apollo hunted and slew Python with a silver arrow. Soon afterwards he

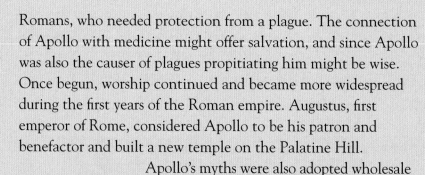

LEFT: A musician and benefactor of civilisation, Apollo was also something of an egomaniac who would tolerate no rivals.

acquired another of his signature items, the lyre, by roundabout means. Mercury stole Apollo's cattle and hid them in a cave, quite possibly just for the sake of stirring up trouble. Apollo asked Jupiter to intercede, and Mercury was instructed to give back the cattle.

However, Mercury must have become bored while hiding in a cave with only a herd of cows for company, for he hit upon the idea of killing a tortoise and fashioning it into a musical instrument. From the shell of the unfortunate tortoise he made a lyre, stringing it with the creature's entrails. This improvised musical instrument must somehow have produced pleasing sounds, because when Apollo came to collect his cattle he decided he wanted the lyre instead.

Apollo naturally became the greatest lyre player – and indeed the greatest musician – in the universe, and was exceptionally proud of it. When the rustic god Faunus began to claim his music rivalled that of Apollo himself, Apollo felt the need to prove him wrong. Faunus played his pipes and Apollo the lyre, and while Faunus made music that brought birds and animals to hear it, Apollo's music caused the whole world to stop and listen. Everyone agreed that Apollo was the superior musician, except for King Midas of Phrygia. Apollo was so annoyed at this error of judgement that he cursed Midas to have the ears of a donkey.

Apollo would not forgive any challenge to his pre-eminence as a musician. When the satyr Marsyas claimed to be better, Apollo defeated him in a contest and cruelly punished Marsyas. The satyr was hung up on a tree and flayed of his skin, which Apollo then tied to the tree. It is notable that while Apollo was worshipped as a bringer of peace and order, he was not particularly benevolent. As with the Pax Romana imposed by the empire, Apollo's peace was protected by the threat of horrible violence.

Apollo had many lovers, and some of the female ones bore him children. His son Asclepius brought the science of medicine

ASPECTS AND EPITHETS

The Roman deities sometimes had numerous aspects, or were known by different names. The goddess Lucina was probably not a separate being, but was instead an aspect of Juno in her role as midwife. Diana is also sometimes known as Lucina, as she assisted in the birth of her brother Apollo. Thus when Juno 'imprisoned Lucina', this can be interpreted as Juno withholding her assistance by suppressing that aspect of her personality.

to the world and Orpheus was a famous musician. His other children included city-founders and oracles. Among Apollo's male lovers were Adonis, the most beautiful man in the world, and King Admetus of Pherae.

Diana

Diana was the firstborn twin of Apollo, product of the union of Jupiter and the Titan Latona. She is associated with nature and hunting, and with the use of the bow. She existed on the fringes of civilization or just beyond them, and as such governed the boundaries of the world such as the edges of the tamed lands around a city and the borders between the world of the living and that of the dead. Her Greek counterpart is Artemis, with whom she shares a near-identical mythology.

It is likely that the worship of Diana began in pre-Roman Italy, with later Greek influences. In Roman times she was part of a divine triad with Egeris and Virbius, a water-nymph and minor woodland god respectively, and was also worshipped in three aspects. These were her connections with the moon, with the underworld and with nature and hunting. Diana never married or took a lover, and was revered as a patron and protector of virgins.

Diana was born fully adult, as already discussed, and able to help with delivering her less developed brother Apollo. In some versions of the story Apollo grew to adulthood in a few days and hunted Python, the monster sent by Juno to harass Latona. Other variants have the twins, both armed with magical bows, engaged in a long hunt before slaying it near Delphi. Although Diana and Apollo

BELOW: Apollo and Diana supported one another's early career, but while Apollo embraced civilisation Diana preferred to live in the wilderness.

made an effective team, their natures were very different. Apollo gravitated to civilization whereas Diana preferred the wilderness. She generally had little to do with mortals or other gods, preferring the company of her band of nymphs.

Like the other Roman gods, Diana was proud and unforgiving. When Actaeon, hunting stags in the forest with his hounds, accidentally caught sight of Diana bathing in a stream she punished him savagely. Splashing the hunter with water from the stream, the goddess turned Actaeon into a stag. He retained his human identity even though his form had changed, but all his hounds saw was a stag. Actaeon was chased down and killed by his own pack.

Minerva

Minerva was the child of Jupiter and a Titan named Metis. During the pregnancy, Jupiter became concerned that mythology would repeat itself. As Caelus had been overthrown by Saturn and Saturn by Jupiter, so might it be with Jupiter and this new godling. Jupiter attempted to solve the problem in a similar manner to Saturn, but instead of eating the babies he devoured Metis with Minerva still in her womb.

Whereas Metis was slain, Minerva somehow survived and eventually made her way inside Jupiter's head. Some versions of

RIGHT: **Minerva was a highly effective military leader, personifying the organisation and careful planning that made Rome's war machine so effective.**

her tale have her springing forth from Jupiter's forehead, fully armed, and others state that Vulcan smashed Jupiter's head open with an axe to free the goddess. Rather than overthrowing her father, Minerva took her place alongside him as part of the Capitoline Triad. She never married or took lovers.

Minerva is associated with intellect, craftsmanship and art, as well as both war and peace. She was revered as a patron of civilization and civilized endeavours, and also as the warlike protector of society. Her wisdom and intellect permitted her to overcome threats that were beyond the mere violence of Mars, and her displacement of Mars in the ruling triad reflects the development of Roman society.

Worship of Minerva began with the adoption of an Etruscan goddess named Menvra. Greek influence resulted in the goddess morphing into a counterpart to Athena and the adoption of her myths. Later, as the expanding influence of Rome began to require more planning and organization, Minerva became one of the most important Roman deities. The Roman civilization can fairly be said to have adopted rather than developed most of its mythology and technology, but what the Romans were especially effective at was putting ideas into practice. Minerva can be seen as the personification of this genius for organization.

Mercury

Mercury was the child of Jupiter and the nymph Maia. He found a niche as the messenger of the gods but was also responsible for commerce and travel. This included the transit of mortal souls into the underworld, and Mercury was the only god able to move freely in and out of that realm. He was not especially trustworthy, representing thieves as well as merchants, and used his status as a messenger to his own advantage.

Worship of Mercury began in the third century BCE. He was probably originally an Etruscan deity named Sethlans, but the cultural influences

BELOW: Mercury is primarily known as a messenger, but he was also the patron of merchants and thieves.

of the time were such that the Romans essentially adopted
Mercury as the Greek god Hermes with a name change. His
status as a messenger and go-between translated into a position
as an instrument of cultural assimilation. Various non-Roman
peoples are described as 'worshipping Mercury' when in all
likelihood they had never heard of him. By conflating the Roman
Mercury with a locally worshipped god a major obstacle to
pacification of conquered peoples was removed. In this, Mercury
admirably fulfilled his role as a somewhat deceptive facilitator of
communication.

Mercury was something of a troublemaker, sometimes creating
disturbances just for the sake of it, but he was also a valuable
asset to Jupiter and the other gods. He was the one who found
Proserpina in Pluto's underworld, and was sent by Jupiter to
extract the nymph Io – when she was a heifer – from under
the watchful gaze of Argus. The myths of ancient Rome are
full of stories where the power of the gods and the necessity of
obedience to them are central to the tale – the morality taught

ABOVE: **Mercury
sometimes acted as a
hatchet-man for Jupiter.
Murdering Argus rather
directly solved the
problem of how to get
Io out from under his
watchful gaze.**

by such myths is one of subordination to authority rather than 'doing the right thing'.

Venus

Venus is sometimes described as the child of Jupiter, but more commonly she is said to have resulted from the castration of Uranus by Saturn. Flung into the sea, fragments of Uranus's genitals somehow impregnated the ocean, from which Venus emerged. She is associated with all aspects of love – physical attraction, sex and the love of family.

BELOW: Botticelli's 'Birth of Venus', painted around 1495, is the most widely known depiction of the goddess.

Venus is known to have been worshipped in the third century BCE, and may have been revered before that. Like most Roman deities she has a Greek counterpart – Aphrodite – with whom she shares most of her mythology. She is credited with being the mother of Aeneas and thus the ancestor of Romulus. Julius Caesar later claimed descent from the goddess.

As might be expected of the goddess of love, Venus had a complex and varied set of relationships. She was married to Vulcan, god of fire, but had no children with him. Her affairs with Mars produced twin deities Concordia and Metus – associated with harmony and terror – and Timor who personified fear. The Cupids, who did Venus's bidding by shooting love-arrows at whoever she directed, also emerged from this union.

Venus also had numerous other male and female lovers. Among them was Mercury, with whom she produced a child named Hermaphraditios who was both male and female. Mercury also interfered in the affairs of Venus and Mars. On one occasion he informed Vulcan of his wife's infidelity, which seems a little hypocritical. However, this does illustrate a philosophy running through all of Roman mythology – essentially, the power or capability to take an action makes it acceptable to do so. This may reflect the internal politics of early Rome, where power was far more important than benevolence. On this occasion, Mercury's tattling produced a

VENUS ALSO HAD NUMEROUS OTHER MALE AND FEMALE LOVERS. AMONG THEM WAS MERCURY, WITH WHOM SHE PRODUCED A CHILD NAMED HERMAPHRADITIOS WHO WAS BOTH MALE AND FEMALE.

result. Determined to catch the lovers in the act, Vulcan forged a net so fine as to be invisible but strong enough to ensnare even Mars. He placed the net over the bed he supposedly shared with Venus and in due course she was entangled along with her lover. The other gods were summoned and ridiculed the pair, but in all likelihood this was as much about having fallen for Vulcan's trap as any judgement of their morality.

Vulcanus

Vulcanus, or Vulcan, was the child of Jupiter and Juno, an auspicious beginning that was followed immediately by disaster. The child was insufficiently attractive for his mother to find acceptable, so she flung him away. Depending on the variant of the story, Vulcan may have been born lame or become so as a result of tumbling down Mt Etna.

The baby god was rescued by nymphs, who raised him in concealment under Mt Etna. Vulcan became a great smith, using the fires of the volcano to create magical treasures of great beauty and power. Eventually the gods learned of his talents, and Vulcan earned a place among them by creating Jupiter's sceptre and lightning bolts, Mercury's winged helm and other powerful items. As a result he became associated with fires, particularly forges.

Worship of Vulcan began very early in the history of Rome, probably some time in the eighth century BCE. This may reflect the importance of forging and craftsmanship to the developing city – Rome attracted crafters and experts who might not be so welcome elsewhere for whatever reason, and benefited greatly from their talents. The concept of a lame blacksmith is also ancient. Many cultures deliberately crippled their smiths to prevent them from taking their talents elsewhere. Some time after worship began, Greek influences provided Vulcan with a mythology shared with his Greek counterpart Hephaistos.

Vulcan never forgave his mother for rejecting him, and even though he had created a place for himself among the gods he lacked many of their attributes. Most of the gods were beautiful and powerful in their own right, whereas Vulcan, who was considered deformed, fell victim to prejudice and had to work

OPPOSITE: **Venus visits her husband at his forge. Although his cleverness won Vulcanus a wife, it did not bring about a happy marriage.**

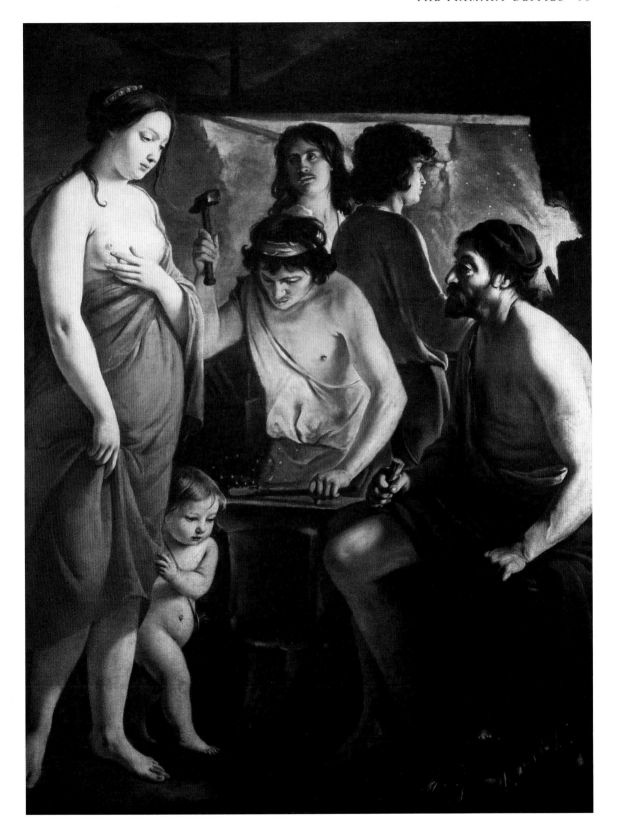

ABOVE: Both Greek and Roman mythologies contain the same story of the birth of Minerva (or Athena). Vulcanus frees the goddess from her father's head, whilst in the background other gods act according to their nature.

at godhood. He was clever, though, and plotted to improve his position through the inventive use of divine gadgetry.

Vulcan desired Venus as much as everyone else did, and wanted her for his wife. Knowing he had no chance of even a passing affair, Vulcan resorted to politics rather than romance. He made a wonderful chair for his mother, Juno, who probably should have known better than to accept a gift from a rejected son who spent his days making magical treasures. Sure enough, once she sat in the chair she became ensnared.

Vulcan refused to release Juno unless he was given the hand of Venus in marriage. Jupiter agreed and ordered Venus to marry the forge god. It is notable that although Jupiter had the power to command all the gods, he chose to force Venus to marry Vulcan rather than demanding the release of his wife. In any case, the marriage was not a happy one. Venus by her very nature was incapable of fidelity and chose to spend her time with powerful lovers such as the god Mars or the mortal Adonis, who was the most beautiful man in the world.

Vulcan was a facilitator rather than a doer, providing the gods with their magical treasures but never embarking on adventures of his own. Nevertheless, he is central to the Roman pantheon as a source of power for the other gods and the instigator of plots such as his ensnarement of Mars and Venus. In some versions of the tale he acts as a sort of violent midwife to his half-sister Minerva, hacking open the head of Jupiter to allow the goddess to escape.

Mars

Mars is often considered to be the child of Jupiter and Juno, though some versions of the myth name Juno as sole parent. Either way, he was rather more favoured than his brother Vulcan. He is associated with violence and warfare of an unsophisticated sort, and appears to be a straightforward sort of god. Unsurprisingly, perhaps, he was a lover of Venus, with whom he had several children. His disregard for his own marriage and Venus's relationship with Vulcan is entirely in character and typical of powerful Roman individuals.

Mars married Anna Perenna, a nymph who may have originally been a woman from Carthage. According to some versions of the tale, the mortal Anna Perenna was the sister of Queen Dido of Carthage. She journeyed to Italy, where she incurred the jealousy of Aeneas's wife Lavinia. To escape her wrath Anna flung herself into the river Numicius. Anna Perenna became a nymph associated with the river and ultimately a goddess of time.

Not all of the lovers of Mars were willing. Desiring Rhea Silvia, who had been forced to become a vestal virgin, Mars

BELOW: Despite both being married to others, Venus and Mars produced several children including the Cupids who served Venus thereafter.

raped her and thus fathered Romulus and Remus. The Roman cultural psyche seems to have been far more interested in the divine connection than how it came to be, perhaps reflecting the philosophy that obedience to the will of the gods was of paramount importance.

Worship of Mars began very early in the history of Rome, though he may have been known by other names at first. His place in the Archaic Triad was assured by the need of society for a war god who could protect and advance the interests of

the Roman people in a troubled time. Over time, the ferocious Mars was edged out by the more calculating Minerva. The rivalry between Mars and Minerva is reflected in an alternative version of his origin myth. In this variant, Juno was jealous of Jupiter's achievement in being a sole parent to Minerva. This is slightly misleading, because Jupiter fathered Minerva with the Titan Metis in the usual manner, then ate her while she was pregnant. Juno, on the other hand, truly was Mars' only parent. Using a magical flower given to her by the goddess Flora, Juno became

pregnant without the involvement of anyone else and in due course gave birth to Mars.

The relationship between Mars and Minerva was not always adversarial. At some point he fell in love with his rival, who was determinedly chaste and not receptive to his advances. This brought about an alternative version of the marriage of Mars and Anna Perenna, in which he asked her for help in winning over the reluctant Minerva. Anna Perenna agreed to assist, but deceived the god of war by disguising herself as Minerva. Only when the two had agreed to marry did Anna Perenna reveal her true identity.

The obvious Greek counterpart for Mars is Ares, but the two differ in character. Both are raging warriors, but where Ares causes mayhem and destruction, Mars is usually credited with a positive outcome from a conflict. This may reflect differences between Roman and Greek society. Rome had something of a national identity, and wars that benefited Rome benefited all her people. On the other hand Greece was a collection of city-states. A war that benefited one inevitably harmed another. Thus their war gods are fundamentally different in character – Ares caused chaos whereas Mars brought peace and prosperity through the application of violence.

THE OBVIOUS GREEK COUNTERPART FOR MARS IS ARES, BUT THE TWO DIFFER IN CHARACTER. BOTH ARE RAGING WARRIORS, BUT WHERE ARES CAUSES MAYHEM AND DESTRUCTION, MARS IS USUALLY CREDITED WITH A POSITIVE OUTCOME FROM A CONFLICT.

LEFT: **Mars was eclipsed by the more calculating and sophisticated Minerva, reflecting a move from tribal conflicts to the politico-military strategy of the Roman state.**

3

LESSER DEITIES AND MAGICAL BEINGS

Along with the *Dii Consentes*, eight additional gods and goddesses made up the *Dii Selecti*. All aspects of daily life and state endeavour were governed by these or a host of lesser gods, and other supernatural beings also feature in Roman mythology.
These include monsters, magical creatures and semi-divine heroes.

To a modern observer it can seem like the mythology of any ancient culture was unchanging and always existed in the form we now associate with it. This is not the case, however. Beliefs changed over hundreds of years and from place to place. One consequence of this is the existence of multiple versions of the same god's stories, some of which can be contradictory, or of gods who seem to have the same purpose and area of influence.

Roman gods and mythical creatures were mostly derived from Greek and Etruscan traditions, but others might be co-opted

OPPOSITE: **An 1847 depiction of the decadent lifestyle of later Romans. Mythology changed along with the society that created it.**

wherever they were found. The mythology of ancient Rome evolved over time, with creatures and beings added for no other reason than they were necessary for the backstory of a god who was now worshipped as if they had always been part of the Roman pantheon.

The names of many Roman deities can seem familiar even if we do not know their stories. The usual reason for this is that the deity is a personification of a concept or behaviour that is still known by a word derived from its Latin name. In other cases a god's name or part of it has passed into common usage as a figure of speech or a descriptor. There is a direct correlation between

ANCESTRY OF THE GODS

In the main, the backstories of the Roman gods are carbon-copies of their Greek equivalents. Whatever the origins of a particular deity, Greek influences caused a realignment of myths and stories, which resulted in a near-identical mythology. Some of the Roman gods may originally have had a different ancestry or origin story, but the adoption and Romanization of Greek mythology created anomalies and contradictions that were best resolved by co-opting the whole mythos.

Thus the ancestry of most Roman deities can be found in Hesiod's Theogony, an epic poem created around 700 BCE that details the origins and interactions of the Greek gods. Sources relating specifically to the Roman pantheon can be difficult to find, and in many cases quote or refer to the Theogony using the Roman deity names either alongside or instead of the Greek ones. This can create confusion over whether a particular name is the Greek or the Roman version. Perhaps it does not matter all that much to the gods themselves – Greek and Roman names were used interchangeably and without undue disaster in some areas controlled by Rome.

LEFT: **A 14th-century copy of Hesiod's Theogony,** which contains the 'origin story' of most of the Greek and Roman gods.

someone 'facing their nemesis' and the goddess of revenge who gave us the word, or between a 'discordant' relationship and the goddess of troublemaking who personified that situation. It would seem that even today the Roman gods continue to personify aspects of human life.

Janus

Janus is associated with doors, of both a physical and metaphorical sort, and with all transitions. He is depicted as having two faces, one looking into the past and the other the future, because the present is the moment of transition between past and future. As the god of portals and doorways, Janus also governed every occasion where someone used one. Making a good entrance, or departing on an endeavour in the right way, might earn Janus's favour and lead to a good outcome.

ABOVE: Janus is depicted with two faces; one looking to the future and one into the past.

Janus is unusual in being a truly Roman deity. Worship began in the earliest days of the city or perhaps before, with little or no outside influence on the development of his mythology. In one version of his myth, Janus assisted the early Romans against the Sabines. Understandably angry at the carrying-off of their women, the Sabines attacked Rome but were driven off by a jet of hot water from the temple of Janus. Thereafter the doors of the temple were left open, allowing the god to come out and assist the city at need.

In another version of Janus's story he was apparently a mortal man at first. Exiled from Thessaly, Janus settled in Latium and there, with his wife Camasnea, he raised his children. One of them, named Tiberinus, became the god of the nearby river, which was henceforth known as the Tiber. Janus built a city close to the river and had good relations with Rome. When Saturn was overthrown, he found refuge with Janus. This ushered in a golden age of prosperity for the region, and Janus was deified on his death.

Janus was important to every undertaking and journey, but especially so to the army of early Rome. At the beginning of a campaign the army symbolically departed through the temple doors, which were to be left open until the victorious force returned. In practice, there was always a campaign going on somewhere so it was rare for the doors to be closed. This did occur in 48 BCE, when the temple doors were closed in a great ceremony honouring the deeds of Julius Caesar. The symbology was powerful – the Roman world was now finally at peace thanks to Caesar, and Janus's assistance would not be needed for a while.

The minor god Portunes is associated with Janus, because Portunes governs keys and doors of both a physical and metaphysical sort. Thus as well as the obvious opening and

BELOW: The closing of the temple doors was ordered upon a few occasions after 48 BCE, symbolising an end to a conflict and the beginning of a period of peace.

closing of portals, Portunes is also associated with seaports because they give access to the sea and the land, and in a more general sense with 'getting inside' in the appropriate manner. Today, someone who is overly persistent in their requests or questions may be described as importunate – Portunes would not approve of their methods of getting to the information or obtaining the response they desire.

Genii

In early Rome, the Genii were local minor deities or spirits, associated with a household and representing the male head of the house (Genius) and the female head (Iuno). These were not the souls or spirits of the people themselves, but a guardian spirit representing their role and status. The nature of Genii changed over time, and they became associated with individuals rather than a position in the household. People who were not heads of a house, and even gods, began to be perceived as possessing a Genius. Over time, the concept of Genius was extended to locations and organizations, and even to the

RIGHT: **The Lares began as minor gods connected with cultivated areas, but morphed into a personification of a particular family's household.**

THE *DII SELECTI*

The *Dii Selecti* are the 20 most important gods, although in some cases the deity listed is a category. Genii, for example, are spirits or minor divinities of local importance. This place within any given individual's *Dii Selecti* would be taken by a household spirit or the Genius of an organization such as close associates in business or among soldiers.

In addition to the 12 major gods, the *Dii Consentes*, the *Dii Selecti* was composed of:

- Janus – god of portals
- Sol – god of the sun
- Luna – goddess of the moon
- Saturn – a Titan or primal god of the sky
- Tellus – a Titan or primal goddess of the earth
- Orcus – a god of the underworld, possibly an aspect of Pluto
- Liber – a god of wine, later identified as Bacchus
- Genius/Genii – local or personal gods

Roman state as a whole. The gods themselves were considered to possess Genius, representing their inner being and true nature in the same manner as a human.

A person's Genius was considered divine rather than mortal, even though it lived and died with the individual. Paying respect to someone's Genius was a high honour, because it implied their true nature was far above the norms of humanity. The concept of Genius may have paved the way for worship of the emperors when they were still alive, though that may have had as much to do with the demands of certain emperors as any mythological logic. The emperor Augustus was offered worship while he was still alive and opposed the practice, but it was perfectly all right to worship his supernatural Genius.

Gods of natural phenomena

As with many polytheistic religions, the Romans recognized numerous gods associated with natural phenomena. These include actual objects such as the sun and moon, as well as processes such as the transition from day to night. The cycles that governed these transitions were rightly the province of Juno, but the actual phenomenon or object was personified by a different deity.

Among these gods, the most prominent were Sol and Luna, the sun and moon. They were children of Hyperion and Theia, themselves the offspring of Caelus and Tellus. Hyperion and Theia are counted among the Titans rather than being worshipped as Roman deities. Titans were godly beings, and the only real difference seems to be

BELOW: **Luna and Sol, depicted here in carved stone, were among the natural phenomena venerated by the Romans.**

that they belonged to an era before the currently worshipped gods came into their power. Titans usually played little active role in the mythology and served mainly to explain the relationships between the current gods.

Hyperion represented heavenly light and was married to his sister, Theia. She was associated with sight, brightly reflecting gems and metals such as gold. Hyperion and Theia had three children: Luna, Aurora and Sol. Aurora was the goddess of the dawn, and is sometimes said to be the daughter of a Titan named Pallas. Aurora was a minor goddess, notable for her function in beginning the new day and for a sad story in which she phrased a request rather poorly. Jupiter offered Aurora a wish, and she asked for her human lover Tithonus to be immortal. This was granted, but Tithonus continued to age even though he could not die. Aurora eventually turned her aged lover into a cicada.

ABOVE: Like other Titans, Hyperion was acknowledged as a powerful and important being but received little direct worship.

Luna and Sol were more prominent deities, representing the moon and the sun respectively. Both are members of the *Dii Selecti*, the group of 20 most important Roman deities. Worship of the sun, in the form of Sol Indiges, was performed very early in Rome's history, but fell out of favour. The later cult of Sol Invictus, probably resulting from Syrian influences, returned Sol to a prominent position.

Luna was the personification of the moon, and is associated with two other lunar goddesses. Luna was the moon in the heavens and connected with the full moon, whereas the half-moon and the moon on earth were personified by Diana. Trivia, goddess of magic, represented the dark of the moon and the moon in the underworld. These goddesses had connections with fertility and conception, and were thus of great importance to the Roman people. Luna is also credited with governing dreams, the wind and rain, earthquakes and various other aspects of the natural world, including – correctly – tides.

Luna had affairs with Jupiter leading to three children: Herse, Nemeia and Pardia. She appears to have enjoyed Jupiter's favour to such an extent that he bestowed eternal youth on Luna's mortal lover, Endymion. With him, Luna produced 50 children, who became the goddesses associated with the lunar months of a four-year period.

Lesser gods associated with natural phenomena include the four winds. Aquilo was the north wind, Auster the south wind, Vulturnus the east wind and Favonius the west. They were not permitted to take control of the air or the sky, but kept separated each with his own area of interest. The parentage of these wind gods varies depending on the source consulted.

BELOW: The mortal Endymion, lover of Luna, was a rare example of an interaction with the gods that produced beneficial results.

Gods of death and the underworld

Although Pluto was the lord of the underworld, other gods had a role there as well. Notable among them was Proserpina, daughter of Ceres. Proserpina is sometimes considered a death goddess because her absence from the mortal world brings the cold and dark of winter. When she was present in the underworld she shared a palace with Pluto at the entrance of the Fields of Elysium. Pluto himself may have

been a combination of earlier gods, though
sometimes they are mentioned as if they were
separate beings co-existing with Pluto. The
deity Dis Pater (rich father) seems to have
contributed Pluto's overlordship of wealth,
while Orcus punished those who break oaths.
Orcus and Dis Pater appear to have been
combined at some point, though they do seem to
have had separate origins.

The souls of the dead were immortal, and could
at times leave the underworld. Known as Dii manes,
these spirits were propitiated in formal ceremonies held
at various times of the year. Accounts vary as to whether
all dead souls became manes, or if they could become
other types of spirit depending on how good, bad or
indifferent the individual was.

In some accounts, the terms lares and
manes seem to be used interchangeably, but
on other occasions there are distinctions.
Lares, in these cases, are particularly notable
manes who have been elevated to the status of heroes or
minor gods. Among them are the lares domestici, the most
important spirits associated with a particular household, and
the lares publici, who had a wider remit. These might be the
protectors of a city or a district within it. Lares might also be
associated with a rural area or a particular concept, such as
travelling on a road.

The goddess Libitina presided over funerals, and her name
became a byword for death. Within the temples of Libitina
were stored everything necessary for a proper funeral and burial
or cremation of the deceased. Ensuring that funerals were
properly performed was important for society as a whole, because
souls that could not cross the River Styx for lack of suitable
ceremonies might cause trouble in the mortal world.

Dea Tacita was another goddess associated with death. She
personified 'fear of obscurity' – being forgotten after one's death
– and Mors was the personification of death itself. She was said
to bring about the end of a person's life when their time arrived,

ABOVE: By the time of
Emperor Augustus, it
was the custom to have
two statuettes of Lares
in a house, both holding
a drinking vessel and an
offering dish.

regardless of their status or worldly cause of death, while the minor deity Viduus was responsible for separating the soul from the body.

Gods of food, wine and indulgence

In the earliest days of Rome, the god Liber – also known as Liber Pater, or 'free father' – was associated with Ceres, an agricultural goddess, and also with Libera. The latter seems to be a female equivalent of Liber, but may have originally had a different identity. As Rome became a republic, Liber's worship was made official. He was a patron of the plebian classes, protector of their freedoms despite the restrictions put in place by the higher social strata.

The worship of Liber was heavily influenced by the Greek Dionysus, whose mythology was adopted along with elements of his identity. This created the god Bacchus, the patron of altered mental states arising from drunkenness, religious fervour or inspiration. Whereas Liber encouraged unrestrained conduct when under the influence of wine, Bacchus was a rather more exuberant god associated with extremes of behaviour and wild festivities.

In his new mythology, Bacchus was born twice. The first time was as a son of Jupiter and Proserpina. Jupiter assumed the form of a snake and crept into the underworld to see Proserpina, with whom he appears to have fallen suddenly, deeply and temporarily in love. Their child was Liber. He fought alongside Jupiter and the other gods against the Titans, but was brutally slain. Jupiter was only able to salvage Liber's heart, but from it he

BELOW: **The wild Bacchus replaced the earlier, more strait-laced, Liber as the god of wine and indulgence.**

created a potion that enabled Liber to live again. The potion was given to Semele, a mortal woman married to the king of Thebes.

Semele became pregnant, but fell victim to Juno's jealousy. Juno caused Semele to fall in love with Jupiter, and a tryst was arranged. However, the sight of Jupiter's true form was too much for a mortal to withstand. Semele was slain by one of Jupiter's thunderbolts. He was able to rescue the infant Bacchus from Semele's womb, however, and in due course the new god joined the Roman pantheon.

The worship of Bacchus included festivals known as Bacchanalia, which have come to be associated with all manner of excesses. It is debatable how accurate Roman writing on the subject is, however, because many Roman commentators were merely repeating what they had heard or deliberately distorting the accounts to suit their own agenda. Bacchus was still a plebian god, who encouraged civil disobedience and intemperate behaviour. The disapproval of writers patronized by the noble classes seems inevitable.

BELOW: In 186 BCE the Senate forbade Bacchanalia on moral grounds, though it is debatable of effective this measure might have been.

More temperate deities presided over food and drink, even at lavish banquets. Bibesia was the goddess of drink, and if properly honoured would ensure the wine or other drink was good and well-received. Her counterpart was Edesia, who performed the same function for food. These were minor gods, but important in their own narrow field of influence.

Gods of nature and agriculture

Roman mythology names many gods associated with nature or aspects of the natural world. Many are quite minor, associated with a particular river or region of terrain, while some had a broader area of influence. Tiberinus was one of the more important of these deities, because he was the god of the River Tiber which flows through Rome itself.

The earth as a whole was represented by Terra, also known as Tellus or Terra Mater. Unlike her husband Caelus, Tellus was worshipped in Roman times, though she became conflated with the 'great mother' goddess Cybele and known by that name. Worship of Cybele began a little before 200 BCE. Although she was originally a goddess of Asia Minor whom the Romans knew of by way of Greek influences, it was the Punic Wars that triggered her incorporation into the Roman mythos.

Under severe pressure from Hannibal's army, which was marauding about Italy threatening the very fabric of the Roman republic, the senate consulted the Sibylline Books. These contained prophecies that could guide Rome through times of crisis, and in this case they spoke of a mother from Pessinus, the centre of worship for

BELOW: Tiberinus would normally have been a minor river god, but his close association with the city of Rome ensured greater recognition.

Cybele. Symbolically importing a meteorite from Asia Minor, the Romans instituted worship of Cybele. Soon afterwards Hannibal retreated from Italy.

Cybele was a goddess of wild nature, but also of agriculture, and was popular with the plebian classes. She had powers to cause and cure diseases and might protect the common folk in time of war. When her worship was imported, she brought with her the tale of Attis. Most sources refer to Attis as Cybele's lover, though he may have been her son. Either way, Attis chose to marry a mortal woman and incurred the wrath of Cybele. He fled but went insane while he was in hiding, castrating himself and eventually dying. Saddened, Cybele asked Jupiter to intercede. Attis became a resurrection god, returning to life in the spring when nature woke from its winter slumber.

The primal goddess Ops was originally associated with the earth's bounty but was, like Tellus, later conflated with Cybele. She was associated with Consus, who may have been the god of grain storage, but his importance waned over time. This may have been associated with the loss of Ops' separate identity. The husband of Ops, Saturn, fared better. Even after being

ABOVE: Cybele, depicted riding a chariot pulled by lions, was an imported goddess who seems to have absorbed earlier deities.

overthrown and replaced as the ruler of the heavens, Saturn retained his importance as the god of agriculture and plenty.

Other gods were responsible for narrower aspects of the natural world, or particular creatures. Flora was a fertility goddess of springtime and flowers. Her worship dates back to the earliest days of Rome and probably long before, showing Greek influences on an already extant Italian cult. Although vitally important to the natural world and those who depended on agriculture, Flora did few great deeds. She did facilitate the birth of Mars, however, by supplying Juno with a magical blossom that would make her pregnant. Thus Juno outdid her husband, who can be considered the sole parent of the goddess Minerva if the involvement of the Titan Metis is discounted. As mentioned earlier, Juno was the only parent of Mars, and it is perhaps fitting that the child of her jealousy was an angry god of war.

FAUNA WAS ANOTHER GODDESS OF NATURE, ASSOCIATED WITH WILDLIFE AND THE SPRING, AND THE TWIN SISTER OF FLORA.

Fauna was another goddess of nature, associated with wildlife and the spring, and the twin sister of Flora. She was the wife of Faunus, who is usually depicted as a fusion of man and goat. He was the Roman equivalent of the Greek Pan, and similarly watched over shepherds. Faunus was a lustful fertility god whose music almost rivalled that of Apollo. He may have started out as Lupercus, a guardian against wolves who was one of the earliest gods worshipped by what would become the Roman people, and evolved into his wider role as a result of Greek influences.

Fauna and Faunus are associated with fauns and satyrs, creatures with the body of a human (almost always male) and a goat's legs and horns. They were Genii, or spirits, associated with woodlands and other rural areas. References to fauns and satyrs are at times interchangeable, but satyrs seem to have been more rumbunctious and likely to cause trouble than the shy fauns. Both liked to play music and have been associated with hidden wisdom, but other accounts state they could communicate only

BELOW: **In this depiction, dating from 100 CE, two satyrs with human legs follow a female worshipper of Bacchus in procession.**

through the most horrendous noises. Accounts also differ on whether fauns and satyrs were mortal creatures touched with a bit of magic or were Genii of nature.

Many gods had an aspect associated with nature or a part of the natural world along with other areas of influence, some of which might be quite different from one another. Diana is commonly known as 'the Huntress' but was also a protector of poor people and slaves. As a fertility goddess, Diana watched over childbirth and helped women conceive. This part of her mythical identity harks back to her role as a midwife for her twin brother Apollo. Similarly, Saturn is associated with crops and agriculture despite a former place as ruler of the heavens.

Social gods

Some deities were associated with social values or concepts, or aspects of daily life. Among the latter was Deverra, who protected a household containing a new baby by driving spirits from the house. Other goddesses associated with childbirth include Carmenta, who was also credited with inventing the Latin alphabet, and Candelifera.

Other deities had a more general area of influence. Discordia governed all forms of discord, including military mutiny and petty acts of spite. Her Greek equivalent is Eris, who triggered the Trojan Wars by causing a dispute among the gods. The shared mythology gives Discordia a place in the founding-story of Rome as the instigator of a chain of events that brought Aeneas to Italy and ultimately led to the creation of the Roman state. In the Roman context, strife was not always bad; a conflict could lead to lasting peace or the furthering of national or personal interests.

BELOW: Carmenta, like many Roman deities, has a variety of differing roles. In addition to watching over midwives and protecting children she is also credited with inventing the Latin alphabet.

The opposite of Discordia was Concordia, goddess of harmony. In particular, Concordia represented cooperation between the plebian and patrician classes in ancient Rome. This was not always the case; not long after the establishment of the republic, the plebians became disaffected with the social situation and effectively went on strike. At this time there was no plebian representation in government and all major businesses were owned by patricians. The plebians' only leverage was the fact they contributed the majority of military personnel, and their refusal to fight for the state was enough to force the patricians to grant concessions. In effect, Concordia represents a social contract whereby all classes contribute to the overall good of the state and receive fair treatment in return.

Concordia also represented harmonious relations and the settlement of disputes in marriages or within households and other social institutions. Another deity important to these institutions was Sancus, originally a Sabine god who governed oaths and agreements, including various aspects of law. Pietas, on the other hand, personified duty rather than sworn or legal obligations. This included duty to the Roman state and the family, but most of all dutiful obedience of the gods. The goddess Pietas gives us the word 'piety'.

The goddess Fortuna presided over luck and fortune, good or bad. Despite their conviction that good fortune was obtained

ABOVE: Although a minor goddess, Concordia was essential to the functioning of Roman society as she secured cooperation between the Plebian and Patrician classes.

propitiating the right gods and ensuring none were offended by any omissions, the concept of luck still played an important role. However, luck was not entirely random. The favour of Fortuna could be gained by being virtuous, though this refers to the virtues of Roman society rather than the modern concept of philanthropy.

Fortuna began as an agricultural goddess. The good fortune of an abundant crop eventually expanded to a broader concept whereby Fortuna offered protection against everything a person could not control. She was popular with merchants and sailors and with gamblers. Fortuna could influence a person's luck – or that of an entire state – and so was worshipped as a household god by many families. There are references to a son of Fortuna named Sors, also associated with luck.

Prosperity could be gained through good fortune or considered an indication of it, but it also had its own dedicated goddess. Named Abundantia, she is rather obscure but would have been important to those wishing to gain or retain a good standard of living. Minor gods of this sort might have been worshipped as household deities in some families, while others honoured different gods more closely tied to their own needs. The goddess Necessitas is associated with destiny, which might be interpreted as luck or fortune rather than an immutable divine roadmap.

The goddess Fides began as a patron of honesty and integrity, in general as well as in terms of the relationship between gods and mortals. Over time her identity changed and her role expanded. She became known as Fides Publica, and came to govern the important documents of the state, including treaties and trade agreements. The temple of Fides Publica became a repository for such documents. Other important pillars of Roman society were Justitia, goddess of justice, whose image remains the personification

ROMAN VIRTUES

The ancient Romans revered Veritas, goddess of virtue. A daughter of either Saturn or Jupiter, depending on the account, Veritas was the mother and patron of the virtues to which a Roman citizen should aspire. These included mercy, hard work and good humour as well as tenacity, avoidance of wastefulness and prudent forward planning. A good citizen was also clean and healthy, honest and had a suitable regard for culture and refinement.

Many of the virtues revolved around how citizens presented themselves to others. Dignity and pride were considered virtues, along with a healthy sense of one's status in society and worth to it. According to many sources the most important virtue of all was dutiful obedience to the will of the gods, though perhaps being seen to possess this virtue was more important to some than actually possessing it.

LEFT: **Veritas personified virtue, but these were Roman virtues and in some cases rather different to those of modern society.**

of justice in many countries to this day, and Libertas who personified liberty.

The Roman goddess of envy was Invidia, invoked when someone coveted another's possessions or was resentful of their achievements. Those on the receiving end of Invidia's attention would mostly feel it was unjust or unreasonable, and might take steps to protect themselves from her ill-favour with amulets in the form of an eye or a phallus.

The passage from childhood to adulthood was of great importance in Roman society, and was presided over by the goddess Juventas who was also associated with the youthful virility of the Roman state as a whole. A young man came of age in his teens, typically between 14 and 17, in a ceremony

ABOVE: The goddess Invidia was invoked whenever someone felt envy of another's achievements or possessions. Wise Romans took steps to protect themselves from her influence.

dedicated to Juventas. He would wear a white toga (*toga virilis*) and take part in a procession to the Forum, where he was formally acknowledged and registered as a Roman citizen. After further observances dedicated to Jupiter the event was celebrated with a feast.

Gods of war and peace

The foremost gods of war were Mars, personifying personal endeavour and glory, and Minerva who guided strategists. Aspects of warfare and the military had their own gods, including Virtus who personified courage and virtue in both a military and a wider context. One of the virtues associated with the military was honour, personified by the deity Honos. The two were often worshipped together. Military commanders had their own goddess of luck named Felicitas, and many soldiers would have worshipped Victoria, goddess of victory. Rome generally saw warfare as a necessity for defence and a means to further

THE EVIL EYE

Invidia was one of the beings associated with the Evil Eye, a concept that exists in various cultures. Someone with the Evil Eye can bring misfortune and harm on others just by gazing upon them. In Norse culture, some legends claim the berserkers possessed the Evil Eye and could blunt their enemies' weapons just by looking at them.

During a Roman Triumph, a phallic icon was placed under the chariot bearing the Triumphant general to protect against the Evil Eye of those jealous of his success. This seems like a wise precaution, because a Triumph was a celebration of astounding achievement that might inspire jealousy in other Romans and would certainly be resented by the captured soldiers marching to their execution as part of the celebrations.

BELOW: **A mosaic from the second century CE, depicting the Evil Eye in a rather literal manner.**

RIGHT: **Nemesis personified doom resulting from divine disapproval, and was also worshipped by soldiers as the goddess of the drill ground.**

the interests of the state – or, commonly, the interests of certain prominent citizens. Thus the wars of Mars and Minerva were ultimately aimed at creating lasting stability, a peace presided over by the goddess Pax. As a daughter of Jupiter and Justicia, goddess of justice, her lineage is a powerful one. Peace, in Roman terms, was the union of strong leadership and unbiased justice.

The goddess Nemesis is typically described as being associated with revenge, which is certainly true of the Greek deity of the same name. However, it is possible that the Roman Nemesis was also concerned with fair rewards. If so, she would visit retribution upon those who deserved it but also helped the worthy receive what was due to them. This was a necessary part of the Pax Romana – fair rewards for those who kept the peace and violent retribution for those who did not.

Borrowed and adopted gods

The original Roman gods were referred to as *indigites Dii*, and were displaced by the *novensiles Dii* – the adopted gods whose mythology over-wrote the original. The *indigites Dii* remained as minor deities and spirits associated with localities or activities. Some of the adopted gods became quintessentially Roman, whereas others retained their original foreign identities.

As Roman influence expanded, the gods of contacted or subjugated peoples were added to the pantheon, sometimes by conflating them with existing deities and sometimes virtually unchanged. Among these was Epona, horse goddess worshipped by the Celtic people of Europe. Epona was not worshipped in republican times, but after the transition to empire – and, more importantly, after the assimilation of large Celtic populations in Gaul and the Danube region – Epona became a Roman goddess. She is also referred to as Hippona.

A distinction can be drawn between 'borrowed' gods such as Epona who were added to the Roman pantheon without much disruption and 'adopted' gods such as Mithras. The latter was probably of Persian origin but morphed into a major member of the later Roman pantheon. Other major foreign gods who were adopted but achieved little real importance include Isis. An Egyptian fertility goddess, Isis was adopted as a 'mystery cult' in some parts of the Roman world and was eventually recognized as an official Roman deity. The cult had many adherents but did

BELOW: The worship of Epona was brought into Roman religion as a result of contact with, and assimilation of, people who venerated her.

ABOVE: **A terracotta statuette of Isis. An Egyptian goddess, Isis achieved minor importance as a 'mystery cult' within the Roman world.**

not achieve the notoriety of Bacchus, another mystery god, nor the importance of Mithras.

The twins Castor and Pollux, sons of Jupiter, are an example of pragmatic veneration of gods. As Kastor and Polydeukes they appear in numerous Greek legends, sailing for a time on the Argo with the heroes Jason and Heracles – the Greek version of Hercules. Roman worship began as early as the sixth century BCE, but the twins were not tremendously important. However, this changed in 484 BCE when two warriors, mounted on fine white horses, appeared at the battle of Lake Regillus and greatly contributed to the Roman victory. Castor and Pollux became associated with cavalry and were given a temple in the Forum.

The origins of the divine twins are not untypical of such heroes. Jupiter had taken a liking to Leda, wife of the king of Sparta. He transformed himself into a swan to seduce her, and in due course she gave birth to an egg containing the divine hero Pollux and Helen, over whom the Trojan War would be fought. She also produced Castor, who was the son of her husband and therefore mortal. Some versions of the tale consider both twins to be divine; others require that Pollux share his immortality with his brother.

Mithras

Mithraism is perhaps the best known of the 'mystery cults' in ancient Rome. Mystery cults varied from conventional religious practices in that they were wholly or partially hidden from outsiders. Whereas most worship and ritual was public – and, indeed, often held on a large scale – mystery religions revealed their myths and practices only to those who had been initiated.

The worship of Mithras began some time in the first century CE. This was widely believed to be the result of Persian influences, but more recent archaeological research suggests the cult may have been of Roman origin. Temples were set up in caves, adorned with a relief of Mithras killing a bull. Beyond this, Mithras remains a mystery of a more mundane sort. There are no known sources describing the mythology of this god, and second-hand accounts are invariably distorted by the writer's lack of knowledge or even bias. What is known was largely discerned from carvings left behind at holy sites, or from passing references in works on other subjects. As a result many misconceptions and partial truths exist.

From carvings at religious sites it appears that Mithras was born from a rock and hunted a bull, riding it until it was exhausted and then slaying it in a cave. He took parts of the animal with him to a meeting with the sun, and the two dined together. Some sites have additional scenes, with Mithras fighting demons and standing over a subjugated demonic enemy. Another site shows the battle of Jupiter and the gods against the Titans.

Other beings are also represented. Mithras is accompanied by two torch-bearers, identified as Cautes and Cautopates. A figure who may be Oceanus, depicted leaning on a rock, appears in some carvings. A lion-headed figure also appears in some carvings, and the gods Sol and Luna are represented. It is possible to concoct all manner of stories from these images, but there is no way to tell for sure what the cult's myths might have contained.

BELOW: Without context, it is difficult to fathom the significance of Mithras' slaying of the bull, nor why Sol and Luna are present.

It seems that the cult was open only to men. It is possible worshippers progressed through seven levels of initiation, each connected with a celestial body or its associated deity. Alternatively, the seven grades may have applied to priests, with ordinary worshippers being initiates. Surviving Byzantine texts suggest that initiation was only available to those who had passed rigorous tests, but the details are impossible to discern. Passage from one level of initiation (or priesthood) to the next was marked with a ritual meal echoing the 'sun banquet' depicted in the temple carvings. Water must also have been important to the rituals, because temples (Mithraea)

ABOVE: **It appears that Mithras defeated various threats and dined amicably with the sun, but whether this represents a reward, an alliance or some other relationship is unknown.**

were mostly constructed near springs or watercourses.

Mithras is, confusingly, often referred to as Sol Invictus, though he is an entirely different deity from the Sol Invictus worshipped as personification of the sun. The cult is also unusual in that its priesthood did not appear to have held state rank. The senior priests of most gods were recognized by the state and were an important part of its structure, but the cult of Mithras appears to have operated on an amateur or popular basis.

The worship of Mithras began at a time when Christianity was just starting to take hold, and Christianity may have been a factor in the decline of Mithraism. There is little evidence of Mithraic worship after 300 CE or so. Interplay between the two religions was inevitable, but attempts to conflate Mithraism with Christian practice have generally been discredited. Apart from anything else, Mithraism was by no means exclusive or at odds with worship of the old Roman deities, whereas Christianity demanded renunciation of all other gods.

Other gods and beings

Some deities are difficult to fit into a single category. Among them are Tranquillitas, goddess of peace and tranquillity. She appears to have been associated with grain, and gained connotations of peace in the sense that society is less troubled when everyone has enough to eat. Somnus, god of sleep, and Muta, a minor deity connected with silence, are other examples of increasingly niche Roman gods. There was even a goddess – Cloacina – associated with Rome's main sewer.

All of these deities were important to those engaged in activities within their area of influence, and any endeavour could be derailed by failing to propitiate an associated spirit or god. Worship was carried out on a pragmatic basis, however. Few people had a need to worship Nemesis on a regular basis, but those hoping to receive what they considered a fair return on their work might, as would someone hoping misfortune might befall an enemy who had done them wrong.

Among the minor gods were the Furies, whose identities, origins and even number vary from one source to another. It is commonly accepted that there were three Furies, but the earliest references do not give a number. Similarly, the popular version of their origins is that when Saturn was castrated his blood fell upon Terra and produced these angry gods. Having established their number as three, later writers gave them identities: Allecto was eternally angry, Megaera was jealous and Tisiphone was dedicated to vengeance on murderers.

The Furies lived in the underworld but came to the mortal earth to punish the wrongdoings of mortals. On the other hand the three Graces made the world a better place by their presence in it. Adopted from Greek mythology the Gratia, or Graces, personified Brightness, Joyfulness and Flowering of a physical and metaphorical sort. Most legends give their number as three but other versions exist. Similarly, the parentage of the Graces varies from one tale to another. The greatest influence exerted over mortals by any deity or group of deities came from

BELOW: The identities of the Furies may have evolved over time, from the personification of a curse or desire for revenge into specific personas each with their own area of interest.

MÉGÈRE   ALECTON   TISIPHONE

OPPOSITE: Psyche was left to die for the sin of being so beautiful the gods became jealous, but was saved by Favonius (also known as Zephyrus), god of the West Wind.

BELOW: As with the Furies, accounts vary as to the actual number of Graces. Later Roman writers stated that there were three and gave them specific remits.

the three Parcae, equivalent to the Fates of Greek mythology. Named Nona, Decuma and Morta, these beings spun the thread of a person's life, laid it out and cut it to length. This process established the events within that life – good and bad – and the person's moment of death. There was nothing a mortal could do about this, and the Parcae do not appear to have been amenable to bribery or worship.

The goddess Voluptas, associated with pleasure, is often described as keeping company with the Graces. She came to be as a result of divine intervention in mortal affairs, in this case originating from the jealousy of Venus. A mortal woman, sometimes known by her Roman name of Anima but more commonly referred to even in Roman mythology by her Greek name Psyche, was the subject of worship that Venus felt should be hers. So great was the beauty of Psyche that her people had forgotten Venus, so naturally she had to be punished.

Venus sent Cupid to shoot Psyche with a love arrow, intending her to fall in love with someone inappropriate or unattractive. However, Cupid somehow bungled the shot and wounded himself, falling in love with Psyche. Meanwhile Psyche's parents, rulers of a human kingdom, had consulted an oracle and were told that Psyche would give birth to a terrifying monster.

Psyche was left to die atop a tall crag, but was rescued by the god of the west wind, who took her to a wondrous house set in a beautiful grove. There, after a magical feast and entertainment she was led to a darkened room where someone she could not see made love to her. This was Cupid, who concealed his identity until foiled by the intervention of Psyche's sisters. They were brought to visit Psyche by the west wind, but were worried that she was pregnant with some kind of monster. The sisters convinced Psyche

to find out the identity of her lover or kill it if it was something dangerous.

Psyche managed to get hold of a knife and a lamp, and when Cupid was asleep she lit the lamp. Instead of a fearsome monster the light revealed the beautiful Cupid, and Psyche was so startled she wounded herself on one of his arrows. This caused her to fall in love with Cupid, but he fled from her.

While Psyche was searching for Cupid, she encountered Faunus and then her sisters. They were jealous of Psyche's magical love-nest and sought to force the wind to carry them there. This was to be accomplished by climbing the crag where Psyche had been abandoned and leaping off, supposedly forcing the wind god to catch them. He did not, and both died at the foot of the crag.

Psyche then entered a temple of Ceres and found it in disarray. Deciding that the gods should be properly worshipped in an orderly fashion, she tidied up the temple and won the favour of Ceres. However, Ceres was not permitted to assist her. Juno similarly was unable to help, so finally Psyche appealed to Venus, who agreed to permit her to serve.

VENUS TOOK THE OPPORTUNITY TO TORMENT PSYCHE, BRUTALIZING HER AND FORCING HER TO UNDERTAKE IMPOSSIBLE TASKS.

Venus took the opportunity to torment Psyche, brutalizing her and forcing her to undertake impossible tasks. Among these was the sorting of a mix of grain and other ingredients flung on the floor by Venus, who then departed for a feast. Assisted by helpful insects, Psyche managed to restore order to Venus's kitchen.

The goddess was not impressed, and sent Psyche on more difficult errands. She was ordered to obtain wool from ferocious sheep belonging to the sun god Sol, from the other side of a dangerous river. Psyche was aided in this task by magical reeds of a sort used to make musical pipes, perhaps indicating assistance from Faunus. She was aided in her second task by Jupiter himself. Ordered to obtain water from the rivers of the underworld, Psyche did her best but was unable to get past the dragons that lived there. Jupiter sent his eagle to fight them, allowing Psyche to succeed.

Naturally Venus was still not satisfied, and sent Psyche to the underworld again. This time she was to obtain some of the beauty of Proserpina. This was just too much, so Psyche climbed

a tower with the intent of jumping to her death. However, the tower was magical and told her where to find the entrance to the underworld, giving instructions on how to make her way through the underworld.

Psyche was successful, and began to return with some of Proserpina's beauty in a box. She decided to look in the box, and was immediately sent into a state of slumber. She was found by Cupid, who had been recovering from his self-inflicted wound in Venus' house and now made his escape. He was able to undo the magical sleep and conveyed the box containing Proserpina's beauty to Venus.

Cupid then made a deal with Jupiter, agreeing to assist when Jupiter desired a mortal woman. In return Jupiter gave Psyche some ambrosia, which rendered her immortal. He then ordered that Cupid and Psyche be married and warned Venus to stop tormenting her. Far from a destructive monster, Psyche gave birth to Voluptas, goddess of pleasure.

ABOVE: Once she had survived the dangers of the underworld, Psyche was able to ask Proserpina for a box containing some of her beauty. It is not clear if Proserpina received anything in return.

ABOVE: Psyche's great beauty offended the gods when she was a mortal, but as a goddess she was favoured with marriage to Cupid.

The legend of Hercules

The legend of Hercules was adopted more or less wholesale from the Greek tale of Heracles, bringing with it additional elements of the Greek mythos such as the half-horse, half-human centaurs and the three-headed dog Cerberus. In the Roman version, Hercules was a demigod, fathered with a mortal woman by Jupiter. This attracted the ire of Juno, who was determined to punish Hercules, presumably because there was little she could

do to her husband to get back at him. Juno's first gambit was to cheat Hercules out of his inheritance. He was to have been king of Mycenae, but Juno prevented his birth until his cousin Eurystheus was born. This placed Eurystheus on the throne and dispossessed Hercules of the kingdom his father Jupiter intended him to rule. Once she allowed him to be born, Juno sent two snakes to kill the infant Hercules. He strangled them and was found happily playing with their corpses.

After this, Juno left Hercules alone for a time but that did not stop him from getting into trouble all by himself. He was taught music by the god Linus, a son of Apollo credited with inventing rhythm and melody. Hercules fell out with Linus and hit him with either a lyre or a stool depending on the version of the story, killing Linus. He would later slay another of his teachers, this time the centaur Cheiron.

Despite this troubled childhood, Hercules married the daughter of the king of Thebes. At this point Juno intervened again and drove him mad. Possessed of god-like strength, Hercules had little trouble murdering his wife and five children, at which point Juno allowed him to regain his sanity and realize what he had done. The tradition of the time was that absolution could be granted by a king, so on the advice of an oracle Hercules presented himself to his cousin King Eurystheus.

Eurystheus agreed to absolve Hercules of his terrible deeds, but only if he completed 10 extremely difficult tasks. This later became 12 when Eurystheus decided Hercules had cheated on two of his labours. The first task was to kill the Nemean Lion, a terrible beast whose hide was impervious to weapons. Hercules bypassed this problem by strangling the lion. Its impenetrable hide served as his trademark garment and armour thereafter. In some versions of the tale Hercules wears the skin of a different lion, which he killed earlier in his career.

Next, Hercules was sent to deal with the Lernaean Hydra, a multi-headed monster sent by Juno to terrorize the region around

BELOW: When Hercules cut off a head of the Lernaean Hydra, it grew two more. He, or perhaps his companion Iolaus, eventually solved this problem by cauterising the stumps.

Hercules' birthplace of Lerna. This was made a lot more difficult by the hydra's ability to grow two heads in the place of every one Hercules cut off. He was assisted in this task by his nephew Iolaus, who cauterized the wounds with fire and prevented new heads from growing. Despite the intervention of a plucky but ill-fated giant crab, which assisted the hydra, Hercules prevailed. Arrows dipped in the poisonous blood of the hydra would become Hercules' weapon of first resort thereafter.

King Eurystheus then sent Hercules to capture the Kerynian Hind, which was sacred to Diana. Killing the animal might have incurred her wrath, so Hercules chased it for months or captured it in a net, depending on the version of the tale. Some variants state that he wounded the hind with an arrow – presumably not one of his poisoned ones – or killed it and then had to explain to the gods that he was acting reluctantly and out of necessity.

After presenting the hind to King Eurystheus, Hercules was sent to capture another fantastic animal. This was the Erymanthean Boar. Again Hercules ran his quarry down after a lengthy chase. He then encountered his old tutor Cheiron, the wise centaur who had taught a number of heroes about medicine. Cheiron was unusual for a centaur, which were mostly bestial and unpleasant. As Cheiron and Hercules were enjoying some wine together, other centaurs arrived. According to some versions of the story Hercules forgot to add water to the wine and the centaurs became drunk. Whatever the cause, a fight broke out and Hercules escalated the matter with this poisoned arrows. One struck Cheiron, mortally wounding the harmless scholar.

Hercules was then sent to clean out the stables of King Augeas, who had so many animals they threatened to bury his city in their droppings. This was a gargantuan task, but just to make it completely impossible Hercules was instructed to complete the cleaning in single day. He accomplished this by diverting rivers to wash the dung away through ditches he dug around the stables.

The next task was to rid the region of Stymphalia of troublesome birds that were harassing and even eating people. They were impossible to catch on the ground because they nested in a vast swamp, and extremely dangerous, with bronze beaks and

WHATEVER THE CAUSE, A FIGHT BROKE OUT AND HERCULES ESCALATED THE MATTER WITH THIS POISONED ARROWS.

THE CENTAURI

The origin of the race of half-human, half-horse centaurs is described in Greek legend, which was apparently adopted by the Romans. The politician and orator Cicero (106–43 BCE) makes reference to the story in some of his writings, and other Roman retellings of the Greek myth also exist. The story begins with King Ixion, who ruled part of Thessaly. Ixion came to Mount Olympus seeking absolution for murdering his father-in-law, and was granted hospitality by Jupiter.

Ixion was rather a bad sort, who in addition to murdering family members, also abused the hospitality of Jupiter by attempting to seduce his wife. Rather than simply preventing the seduction, Jupiter instead created the cloud nymph Nubes (Nephele in the original Greek version) in the likeness of Juno. Ixion raped Nubes, who gave birth to a being named Centaurus. He in turn fathered the race of centaurs on the mares of Mount Pelion.

With the exception of a few civilized individuals such as the scholar Cheiron, the centaurs were a boorish lot, known for their lack of hospitality and tendency to violence. It may be that this reflected the actions of Ixion, and it certainly brought misfortune upon his homeland. Although eventually defeated, the centaurs made war on Ixion's people for some time. Ixion himself was punished by Jupiter by being bound to a fiery wheel which rolled around the underworld.

BELOW: **The centaurs had a noble appearance but were mostly savages who delighted in causing trouble. A notable exception was the ill-fated scholar Cheiron.**

poisonous droppings. Hercules solved the problem by scaring the birds into the air by making a great deal of noise, then shooting them.

Hercules was then sent to deal with a mighty bull that was terrorizing people on the island of Crete. In some versions of the tale this was a magical creature that had recently impregnated the wife of King Minos, causing her to give birth to the Minotaur. Depending on the variant of the tale, Hercules may have slain the bull or brought it alive to Mycenae, after which it escaped and caused a great deal of trouble elsewhere.

ABOVE: **A third-century mosaic of Hercules capturing the Cretan bull. This incident brought other Greek elements such as the Minotaur into Roman mythology.**

More troublesome animals followed. These were the flesh-eating mares of King Diomedes. Various accounts of this task exist. In some, Hercules fought Diomedes and fed his body to the horses. In others Hercules and his friends captured the mares without realizing they were flesh-eaters. On finding his companions dead and half-eaten, Hercules captured Diomedes and fed him to the mares. Ultimately, he was able to bring the animals to King Eurystheus.

Not satisfied with all this dangerous livestock, Eurystheus sent Hercules to capture the girdle of Queen Hippolyta. Leader of the fierce all-female Amazon tribe and a daughter of Mars, Hippolyta had a fearsome reputation, but welcomed Hercules and his companions hospitably. She even agreed to give him the girdle, but Juno derailed the process by telling the Amazon warriors that Hercules was planning to carry off their queen. They attacked, and were defeated, after which Hercules took the girdle anyway.

Next, King Eurystheus sent Hercules to the far end of the Mediterranean, to capture a herd of sacred cattle tended by the three-bodied Geryones. He was assisted by a two-headed dog and a herdsman who was a son of Mars, but they were defeated in a straightforward application of heroic violence. Pausing only to set up what are known as the Pillars

OPPOSITE: **King Eurystheus may not have given sufficient thought to what might happen if Hercules actually succeeded in capturing Cerberus; Eurystheus' terror allowed the hero to declare his tasks were completed.**

of Hercules on opposite sides of what is now the Strait of Gibraltar, Hercules returned to Eurystheus.

These would have been the 10 near-impossible tasks but King Eurystheus decided that Hercules had cheated on two of them. The assistance of his nephew against the hydra was not sanctioned and diverting rivers meant that Hercules did not actually perform the stable-cleaning himself. Two more tasks were assigned.

First Hercules had to journey all the way back to the western end of the Mediterranean, there to locate a magical garden and take from it some golden applies. This was no small task, because the garden was defended by a terrible dragon and in any case was hidden from mortal ken. After receiving guidance from Neptune, Hercules set out and came upon the Titan Prometheus chained to a rock. This was a punishment from Jupiter for stealing the secret of fire from the gods and giving it to humans.

Every day Jupiter's eagle would peck out and eat Prometheus's liver, which regrew in time for the next round of torture. Hercules slew the eagle with one of this poisoned arrows and freed Prometheus, which does not seem to have angered Jupiter. In return, Prometheus told Hercules about his brother Atlas. Atlas was also being punished by Jupiter, this time for fighting against the gods when they took control of the universe. He had to hold the world on his shoulders, a burden Hercules relieved him of in return for obtaining the golden apples. After tricking Atlas into taking up his burden once more, Hercules returned home.

There are other versions of this tale, in which Hercules slew the dragon that guarded the apples and took them or simply asked the guardians of the apples if he could take them while enjoying a friendly meal. However the apples were recovered, Hercules had one more task to accomplish. This would be the hardest yet, for Eurystheus demanded that Hercules go to the underworld and capture Cerberus. This was the three-headed dog who guarded the entrance to the underworld, and a companion of Pluto. Pluto agreed that Hercules could try to capture his hound providing he used no weapons. Using the same trick he had with the Nemean Lion, Hercules strangled Cerberus until he was unconscious and quickly took him to King Eurystheus.

RIGHT: Hercules chose
to end his mortal life
with self-immolation
and ascended to join the
gods. Even Juno finally
stopped harassing him,
accepting the hero as a
new deity.

Eurystheus was terrified of Cerberus, which enabled Hercules
to negotiate from a position of strength. He agreed to take the
hound back to the underworld, if in return the king would accept
the tasks as completed and grant absolution. This done, Hercules
was finally free to live his life as he saw fit. He married Deianera,
daughter of the king of Kalydon, and had a child with her.

Hercules had other adventures, including an incident where
he entered an archery contest organized by the king of Oichalia.
He won, but was refused the prize – the hand of the king's
daughter in marriage – because he already had a wife. Hercules

stole the king's horses, and killed the envoy sent to ask for them back. This was the king's son, and once more Hercules had to seek absolution for his crimes. He consulted the oracle at Delphi but it would not answer, so he stole artefacts, which he hoped would let him set up an oracle of his own. This resulted in a fight with Apollo, protector of oracles, which Jupiter broke up with thunderbolts.

This incident led to Hercules entering the service of Queen Omphale, which aroused the jealousy of his wife Deianera and ultimately led to his downfall. On a previous occasion Hercules had prevented the centaur Nessus from harassing his wife. This was yet another use of the hydra-blood poisoned arrows, resulting in contamination of Nessus's shirt. Nessus persuaded Deianera to keep the shirt and give it to Heracles if she suspected him of infidelity. In due course she did so, and the toxic blood poisoned him. In another version of the tale Deianera was the one poisoned by the shirt, after which Hercules did not want to live any longer. Either way, Hercules built a funeral pyre for himself and from it ascended to join the gods.

The legend of Hercules adds a great deal to the Roman mythos, and ties in with various Greek myths that were otherwise of no real importance to the Romans. The golden apples lay in a garden at the western end of the Mediterranean, in a garden tended by the Hesperides, who were nymphs of the setting sun. The nymphs are, in some accounts, said to be children of Atlas; in others they are the offspring of Nox and Scotos.

The journeys of Hercules tie in to other Greek myths. The Stymphalian birds – those that survived Hercules' onslaught – flew away to find a new home and troubled the Argonauts as they sought the golden fleece. The Cretan bull fathered the Minotaur, which was imprisoned in a labyrinth designed by Daedalus. Daedalus was the father of Icarus, who famously flew too close to the sun and plunged to his death. All of these tales, along with those of Atlas and Prometheus, are connected to the Roman mythos by the story of Hercules, even if they are not explicitly Roman myths. This would have been entirely acceptable to the Romans, who in many ways saw themselves as the rightful inheritors of the best parts of Greek civilization.

THE GOLDEN APPLES LAY IN A GARDEN AT THE WESTERN END OF THE MEDITERRANEAN, IN A GARDEN TENDED BY THE HESPERIDES, WHO WERE NYMPHS OF THE SETTING SUN.

4

ROMAN WRITINGS

Much of what we know about Roman mythology and early history comes from the surviving works of contemporary writers. These individuals set down their works for a purpose, which was not always simply to record what they thought was the truth. Most of the great Roman works were intended to entertain and may have included large elements of propaganda. Since writers were often supported by a rich patron, it is no surprise that many of them felt the need to flatter or create links back to legendary events.

Some of the great Roman writers produced works of what is instantly recognizable as mythology, but even those who were ostensibly writing history or social commentaries might touch on mythological matters or draw on myths to make a point. Modern observers might prefer to separate beliefs and facts, but with

OPPOSITE: In Virgil's *Aeneid,* blind Anchises was rescued from the destruction of Troy by his son Aeneas.

religion such an integral part of daily life that distinction would be all but meaningless to the writers and their intended audience.

Lucius Livius Andronicus (c.284 BCE–c.205 BCE)

Livius is widely considered the father of Roman literature, but was himself a Greek. It is possible that he was a resident of Tarentum and captured as a slave when the city fell to Rome in 272 BCE. He was freed by his owners, thus entering the lowest of free social classes, the freedmen, and became a teacher of Latin and Greek.

What little of Livius's work survives is rather poor, but nevertheless important and influential. He is known to have translated Homer's epic poem *Odyssey* into Latin, beginning a literary tradition and helping popularize Greek mythology among Roman citizens. Romanized as *Odyssia*, the poem tells the story of Ulysses – the Roman name for Odysseus – and his companions as they try to return from the Trojan Wars.

As the first major translation, *Odyssia* can be credited with introducing a number of elements into the Roman mythos. Among these were Polyphemus and the Cyclopes, powerful giants generally assumed to have one eye. In fact, only Polyphemus is described as one-eyed. The Cyclopes captured Ulysses and his companions when they were shipwrecked on Sicily, which may have seemed less plausible to the nearby Romans than the original Greek audiences. By

BELOW: The popularisation of Greek literature brought all manner of supernatural creatures into Roman mythology, often without any significant changes.

clever trickery Ulysses managed to blind Polyphemus and escape with a handful of his companions. Unfortunately for Ulysses, the Cyclopes was a son of Neptune, who cursed Ulysses. For the next 10 years the seas would not permit him to return home. His adventures depleted his ships and men until only he remained, washed up on an island inhabited by the nymph Calypso. He remained there for seven years but turned down the offer of immortality as Calypso's husband. Ultimately, Calypso freed Ulysses on the intervention of Jupiter – by way of a message delivered by Mercury – who requested that Ulysses be permitted to return home.

ABOVE: **Calypso is depicted here taking pity upon Ulysses, though it might be that she acted less out of kindness and more from fear of enraging Jupiter.**

The story of Ulysses could not exist without many other elements of the Greek mythos, so once it became a Roman story all its magical creatures and incredible places became part of the Roman mythological universe. Livius is not solely responsible for this, but given that no earlier translations are known he is likely to be the instigator.

Livius is also known to have translated Greek plays and to have written religious works. Concerned about a series of extremely bad omens, the authorities requested Livius to create a hymn to Juno. This was performed with great ceremony and presumably warded off disaster.

Publius Vergilius Maro (Virgil; 70 BCE–19 BCE)

Better known as Virgil, Publius Vergilius Maro is best known for his epic poem the *Aeneid*. This work ties the mythical story of the founding of Rome in to the Greek legends of the Trojan Wars and sets out many virtues to which a Roman should aspire. Chief among these is obedience to the gods. Virgil's encapsulation of these virtues is remarkable in that his home province of Gallia Cisalpina only became a Roman province in 42 BCE. Virgil witnessed the chaos of the civil wars surrounding

RIGHT: **Virgil is flanked by the goddesses Clio and Melpomene, muses of history and tragedy respectively.**

RIGHT: **Virgil is flanked by the goddesses Clio and Melpomene, muses of history and tragedy respectively.**

the transition from republic to empire and the period of peace and stability ushered in by the final victor, who became the Emperor Augustus.

Virgil's choice of subject matter gave him the opportunity to create a link back to the noble Trojans, whose ruling houses were descended from the gods themselves. This made Rome and her citizens the rightful heirs to the Mediterranean world and worked a new level of gravitas into the founding-story. Within the *Aeneid*, there are many moments of pro-Roman and pro-Augustus propaganda. The divine right bestowed on Aeneas to found and rule a powerful city was also bestowed on his descendants. Likewise there are allusions to events current in Virgil's time, in which Augustus had brought peace to a troubled world.

Drawing heavily on the writings of Homer in terms of style as well as content, the *Aeneid* tells how Aeneas came to Italy with a divine mandate to create a great city. Aeneas was the child of Venus and her mortal lover Anchises. His father was a member of the Trojan royal family, and the boy grew into a semi-divine hero. Despite this and the assistance of the gods, the Trojans were besieged by a huge Greek army and ultimately their city fell. Aeneas might have been inclined to fight to the last, but he was told of a prophetic vision in which he journeyed to Italy. This would ultimately lead to the creation of a new centre of power, ensuring that Trojan greatness would endure.

This was not to the liking of Juno, who sent a storm to wreck Aeneas's ships. In some versions of the tale Venus asked Jupiter to help her son; in others Neptune was offended that Juno was intruding into his area of influence and calmed the storm. Either

BELOW: Virgil reads his *Aeneid* at the court of Emperor Augustus, apparently causing quite a sensation.

ABOVE: **The sudden appearance of a fleet filled with displaced Trojans may have alarmed Queen Dido, but her meeting with Aeneas flowered into romance rather than conflict.**

way, Aeneas was forced to make landfall at Carthage to repair his vessels.

In Carthage, Aeneas fell in love with its queen, Dido. Aeneas' reluctance to leave her in order to complete his mission may reflect the role Carthage played as a major enemy of early Rome, but rather than a foe or selfish distraction, Dido is represented as a tragic victim of circumstances. It may be that her suffering was intended to be inspirational in a way – the gods were obeyed and the greatness of Rome resulted. This devotion to pious duty regardless of personal cost was a Roman virtue, and the tale of Aeneas may have been intended to serve as an example to follow.

Aeneas intended to stay with Dido but was reminded of his duty by Mercury. He set out once again and was beset by storms. Aeneas asked for aid from Neptune and this was granted, but at a price. Neptune took Palinurus, Aeneas's helmsman, in return for his assistance. The sacrifice of a great sailor in return for the safe passage of the ships is typical of Roman religion – the gods will help mortals but will always want something in return.

Landing in Sicily, Aeneas encountered the Sibyl, who prophesied that he would be successful despite many troubles along the way. She told Aeneas how to enter the underworld and there he encountered some of the casualties his fleet had suffered since leaving Troy. They were unable to cross the river Acheron and complete their journey into the underworld because they had not been properly buried, but Aeneas was assured that their bodies would be found and buried by kindly strangers.

After meeting his helmsman Palinurus and having an unpleasant encounter with Dido, who killed herself in grief when Aeneas left her, Aeneas visited Tartarus, where the worst of mortals were sent to suffer. After this Aeneas entered the rather

SIBYL IN ROMAN MYTHOLOGY

The first appearance of a Sibyl occurred in Greek mythology. This was a single individual, an ancient woman who told the future through incoherent prophecies. This original character was named Sibylla and located in Asia Minor, but over time the term Sibyl became a title and was applied to oracles and prophets of a similar sort all over the Mediterranean world.

In addition to the Sibyl encountered in Sicily by Aeneas, others feature in Roman mythology. Dionysius of Halicarnassus relates how the Roman king Tarquinius Superbus was offered books of prophecy by the Sibyl located at Cumae. Tarquinius Superbus considered the price too high, so the Sibyl burned six of the nine books before Tarquinius Superbus agreed to buy the remaining three for the same price as the original nine. The books were held in the temple of Jupiter, to be consulted when Rome was in great need.

LEFT: **Trying to bargain with the Sybil proved counterproductive, as Tarquinius Superbus discovered to his cost.**

more pleasant Elysium. There, he met his father Anchises, who introduced Aeneas to future great Romans, including Julius Caesar and Romulus. Anchises spoke of the future greatness of Rome, though what was prophecy in the poem was of course history to the readers.

Finally, Aeneas landed in Latium and was well received by its king. Other cities and tribes nearby were less welcoming – notably the Rutuli. This was partly because their leader wanted to marry Lavinia, daughter of King Latinus. Her marriage to Aeneas was to be part of an alliance between Latium and the

new arrivals, which the Rutuli sought to prevent by force of arms. With assistance from the Etruscans, Aeneas was victorious and the alliance went ahead.

The followers of Aeneas founded a city named after his new wife. Lavinium was the parent city of Alba Longa, where in due course the twins Romulus and Remus would be born. Thus Virgil added a great deal of backstory to the founding myth as well as working in retroactive prophecies about the development of Rome. Essentially he was saying that what had happened had always been destined to happen, and that so long as Romans were dedicated servants of the gods they would be the rightful rulers of the mortal world.

The complexity of the *Aeneid* is considerable, to say the least. Any such story must be consistent, even when dealing with capricious gods. In the original Greek version Athena made advances towards Paris, ruler of Troy, and plotted against the city when she was rejected. In the Roman version, Athena's place was taken by Minerva, meaning that Virgil had to solve the problem of how the goddess went from causing the destruction of Troy to protecting its successor.

The solution was determined and dedicated reverence from Aeneas, even when Minerva was trying to kill him. When he escaped from the fall of Troy he took with him a statuette of the goddess, keeping it safe throughout his adventures. Ultimately Minerva was won over by Aeneas's devotion and ceased to be angry with everything Trojan. Indeed, she would become the war-goddess who presided over the Roman conquest of the known world. The statuette was placed in the temple of Vesta, and according to legend Rome could never fall if it remained safely there.

The *Aeneid* features a different kind of heroism from most modern adventure stories, or even the Greek epics it drew on. Virgil's protagonist is a hero of duty rather than self-will. He prevails by doing what the gods want him to do rather than imposing his own choices on the world. In this, Aeneas is not so much a heroic captain of his own fate as an instrument of divine will. A more conventional protagonist might have chosen to raise Carthage to greatness, challenging the very gods with his great love at his side, but this was not the tale Virgil wanted to tell or behaviour he wished to encourage. Instead the message of

BELOW: **The apotheosis of Aeneas, painted by Jan van Neck in 1683.**

the Aeneid is that success comes to those who obey the gods, and true heroism is found in being willing to pay the great price.

Quintus Horatius Flaccus (Horace; 65 BCE–8 CE)

Despite humble beginnings as the son of a freedman, Horace was educated in Rome and served in the army during the civil wars following the assassination of Julius Caesar. He won high honours, but was on the losing side. Nevertheless, Horace was able to return to Rome, where he earned an introduction to a group of influential writers and ultimately the Emperor Augustus.

The work of Horace focused heavily on moral issues, praising the virtues of those who lived a moral life and attacking social ills that resulted from immoral conduct. He also published his *Odes*, collections of poems in the Greek tradition, and *Epistles*. The latter were rather subdued works containing Horace's thoughts on the nature and value of poetry, along with commentary on the literary society of Rome at the time.

Late in his lifetime, Horace was the foremost poet in Rome. When Emperor Augustus revived the Secular Games it was

BELOW: Gaius Cilnius Maecenas was a friend of the emperor and patron to poets such as Virgil, Horace and Varius, as depicted here.

Horace who wrote the hymns to
accompany them. The games were an
ancient tradition marking the passing
of one generation into another, and
were originally dedicated to the gods
of the underworld. It is probable that
Emperor Augustus added other deities,
including Apollo and Diana, to those
honoured with the games.

Dionysius of Halicarnassus (c.60 BCE–c.7 BCE)

Dionysius of Halicarnassus migrated
from his home city in what is now
Turkey to Rome, where he served
as a teacher of rhetoric to the
upper classes. This was very much a
necessary skill for anyone wanting to
achieve political success, and brought
Dionysius into contact with a variety
of influential citizens. He eventually embarked on a major work
in the form of *Roman Antiquities*, a history of Rome from its
founding to the beginning of the Punic Wars. This, naturally,
meant narrating myth as history but at that time there really was
no difference as far as most readers were concerned.

ABOVE: Dionysius of
Halicarnassus, depicted
on the title page of
Roman Antiquities.

    Roman Antiquities consists of 20 books, though only fragments
now remain of some of them. The early books narrate the
founding myth of Romulus and Remus, but connect the Romans
back to the Greeks by describing the Greek migrations into Italy
and the voyagings of Aeneas. His aim, stated in the preface to
his work, was to educate the Greeks about the Romans, but there
was an element of propaganda to this 'education'. Dionysius of
Halicarnassus was pushing the idea that the Romans were worthy
successors to the ancient Greeks, perhaps suggesting that the
Roman takeover was not a foreign invasion at all but merely
another round of Greek-on-Greek strife.

    Later books deal with relatively recent history, culminating in
the campaigns of King Pyrrhus of Epirus in Italy. This occurred

in 280–275 BCE, centuries before Dionysius began writing his history. Like the rest of his books, this must have been based on earlier sources and was written with an agenda in mind.

Titus Livius (Livy, 59 BCE–17 CE)

Better known as Livy, Titus Livius is best known for his work *History of Rome from its Foundation*. Little is known about his life, but he did live through some difficult times. His birth province was Gallia Cisalpina, governed at the time by Julius Caesar. Livy witnessed the civil wars that followed the assassination of Caesar, and this seems to have affected his writing. Livy's *History of Rome from its Foundation* contains many references to what he believed to be the cause of all the troubles – immoral behaviour. Thus his work was not merely a recording

RIGHT: Although Livy's work did not generate immediate enthusiasm, it set a new standard for Roman literature written in Latin.

of events; it was a roadmap for avoiding a repetition. Livy differed from other Roman writers in that he was not involved in politics or religion, and had no access to the records stored in the temples. He wrote from a very different perspective – that of an observer of events and their moral underpinnings. Livy was nevertheless a huge influence on subsequent authors. He wrote in Latin, and in a Roman style rather than using Greek or attempting to emulate it. His work was considered rather dry at the time and was not popular, but it did set a new standard for Roman writers thereafter.

Publius Ovidius Naso (Ovid; 43 BCE–17 CE)

Ovid is best known for his *Metamorphoses* and *Ars Amatoria*. Born into an equestrian family, he received a good education and travelled widely, with the expectation he would become a public figure. Instead, Ovid turned his talents to poetry. Much of his early work, including *Ars Amatoria*, was concerned with love affairs and their surrounding complexities. These works were well received, and established Ovid as a heavyweight poet and enabled him to embark on his *Metamorphoses*.

ABOVE: The reason for Ovid's exile remains unknown, but he stated that it was due to an indiscretion rather than a crime.

While writing this great work, Ovid was exiled. The reasons for this are uncertain, but Ovid himself stated that he had committed an indiscretion. It is possible that he revealed too much about the affairs of the Roman elite in his works or spoke about them to the wrong people. The exile was of a rather mild form, which allowed Ovid to retain his property, but he was forced to live out his days on the fringe of the empire.

During this time, Ovid completed his *Fasti*, describing the religious festivals of the Roman year, and finalized *Metamorphoses*. This work posed a challenge for Ovid, because Virgil had redefined the genre with his *Aeneid*. To achieve large-scale recognition Ovid's work had to possess similar levels of artistic merit without merely copying the style. The result

MINERVA WAS OFFENDED AT THE IMAGES OF ARACHNE'S TAPESTRY, AND LAID ABOUT HER WITH HEAVY BLOWS.

was a 15-book collection of tales featuring or centred on the metamorphosis of people, objects and even the universe as a whole.

One tale told in Ovid's *Metamorphoses* concerns the origin of spiders. It came to the attention of the goddess Minerva that a mortal woman was claiming to be as skilled at weaving as she. This sort of arrogant presumption could not be tolerated, but Minerva did give fair warning. Disguised as a wise old woman, she approached the mortal, whose name was Arachne, and suggested she withdraw her claim. When Arachne did not do so, Minerva challenged her to a contest.

One lesson that can readily be learned from Roman mythology is that it is deeply unwise to accept any sort of challenge from the gods, and this occasion was no exception. The disguised Minerva created a tapestry depicting herself becoming the patron deity of Athens, while Arachne recklessly produced one that depicted the gods seducing mortals.

Minerva was offended at the images in Arachne's tapestry, and laid about her with heavy blows. These must have been delivered to the spirit as well as the body, for Arachne fell into despair and attempted to hang herself. At the last moment, Minerva decided not to let Arachne die. Instead she was transformed into a spider

RIGHT: The Roman gods were not kind to those who claimed to rival them. Here, the war goddess Minerva beats Arachne for her presumption.

and cursed to weave forever. Metamorphoses contained tales of the transition of the universe from chaos into its present form, ending with the change from a republic wracked by civil war into the peaceful empire of Augustus. These tales expanded and retold the Greek-Roman myths, presenting the gods as having human-like emotions and desires. Although he never returned to Rome, Ovid influenced writers who came later in terms of style and content. Perhaps his greatest contribution to literature was to record and Romanize the ancient Greek myths that underpinned the whole Roman mythology.

Phaedrus (c.15 BCE–50 CE)

Phaedrus translated into Latin a large body of work attributed to Aesop. The latter was supposedly a Greek scholar but was probably fictional or semi-mythological. Phaedrus was not the first Roman writer to adopt the Greek fables, but his versions of Aesop's tales remained popular into the medieval period. He wrote fables of his own as well as relating the Greek ones, though his most famous work is derived from Aesop. One example is the tale of a fox who cannot reach the grapes he desires so denounces them as sour. Even those not familiar with the story itself will know the modern shorthand figure of speech 'sour grapes'.

BELOW: Phaedrus is responsible for ensuring the survival of numerous classical fables into modern times, adding many of his own to those attributed to Aesop.

Gaius Plinius Secundus (Pliny the Elder; 23–79 CE)

As a young man Pliny the Elder served in the army alongside the future Emperor Vespasian before concentrating on his studies and writing for many years. Later in life he served as procurator – an officer of the treasury – for a time before returning to Rome in 69 CE to take

public office under the new Emperor Vespasian.

Most of Pliny's work is lost, with only his *Natural History* surviving. This was one of the most influential works of all time, serving as a basis for scientific knowledge for centuries after the author's death. This does not mean Pliny's work was entirely accurate, of course. He was recording what he believed to be true but was reliant on the accounts of others for much of his research. Pliny was careful to cite the sources used in compiling his vast body of knowledge.

Although much of Pliny's work was based in observed fact, albeit in places distorted or confused in translation, he did include a number of mythological or fanciful creatures. Other than this, Natural History is a work of science rather than mythology, even where the reported facts-as-Pliny-believed-them came from religious belief rather than observation of the natural world.

Plutarch (46 CE–c.119 CE)

The prolific writings of Plutarch cover a range of topics including essays on historical figures, ethics and philosophy. Like many other Roman writers he wished to foster a better understanding and greater respect between those who saw themselves as Romans and those who identified as Greek. Despite the conquest of the ancient world by Rome, there was still a clear disdain for Roman culture in Greek circles.

Although Plutarch was mostly concerned with topics of the day, his works did touch on the mythology of Greece and Rome. To discuss the possibility that animals engaged in reasoned thought, Plutarch drew on the voyage of Ulysses for an example. Ulysses and his men landed on the island inhabited by the sorceress Circe, whereupon she turned them into pigs. Only Ulysses was protected, thanks to a magical herb given to him by Mercury. Plutarch used this situation as the background to a discussion between Ulysses and one of his transformed crewmembers, in which the pig argued the case that animals do, indeed, reason.

ABOVE: **Although Plutarch was writing on unrelated topics, he used the mythology of the day to get his point across.**

BELOW: **Pliny the Younger was a witness to the eruption of Mount Vesuvius which destroyed the city of Pompeii and killed his adoptive uncle, Pliny the Elder.**

Publius Cornelius Tacitus (Tacitus, 56 CE–c. 120 CE)

Tacitus is rightly renowned as a great historian who created detailed accounts of the Roman empire and wrote a biography of his father-in-law, Agricola. This focused extensively on Agricola's term as governor of Britain in 78–82 CE, and the impossibility of pacifying the tribes of Caledonia. Tacitus did not quite live long enough to be aware of Emperor Hadrian's order in 122 CE to build a wall across Britain. This and other permanent fortifications initiated by Hadrian are often cited as evidence of a 'high tide' of Roman expansion.

Tacitus also wrote the *Germania*, an account of the Germanic tribes outside the imperial borders. This is a factual account as best Tacitus could produce, but contains speculation that there might be a second Pillars of Hercules in the northern seas. Tacitus pondered whether Hercules might have journeyed in the northern lands in the same way he

THE INCLUSION OF THESE WILD TALES DOES DEMONSTRATE A WILLINGNESS ON THE PART OF ROMAN SCHOLARS TO ACCEPT THAT STRANGE AND PERHAPS MYTHOLOGICAL BEINGS STILL LIVED AT THE EDGES OF THEIR ORDERLY WORLD.

might have wondered if a famous Roman or Greek navigator reached a particular location.

This factual account of the Germanic tribes slips over into mythology at the fringes. Tacitus mentions that there are distant tribes with the faces and features of men but the bodies of animals. He explicitly refuses to comment on such unverifiable information, suggesting that he does not believe the tales – or at least he is not willing to speak of such matters in his capacity as a serious historian. However, the inclusion of these wild tales does demonstrate a willingness on the part of Roman scholars to accept that strange and perhaps mythological beings still lived at the edges of their orderly world.

Elsewhere in his text Tacitus tries to make sense of the religious practices of the Germanic tribes and to present them in a manner Romans could comprehend. This inevitably introduces misunderstandings and distortions, because Tacitus or the observers he obtained information from would interpret what they saw in terms of their own knowledge and preconceptions. Indeed, *Germania* provides an insight into just how sexist Roman society was. Tacitus describes the Sitones tribe, and how they are ruled by women. This, he claims, is not merely evidence of a decline below freedom, but even of decent slavery. At least he acknowledges such a land could exist.

Gaius Plinius Caecilius Secundus (Pliny the Younger, c.61 CE–c.113 CE)

An adopted nephew of Pliny the Elder, Pliny the Younger trained as a lawyer and ultimately held high positions in the treasury. He is notable for a collection of private letters on a variety of topics rather than for recording or expanding mythology, but did comment extensively on moral issues connected with current and historical issues. His works provided later scholars with an insight into the daily lives of Roman citizens and the affairs of state.

Appian of Alexandria (c.95 CE–c.165 CE)

Appian of Alexandria was born in the Egyptian city of that name at a time when it was the capital of the Roman province of Egypt. Although he published an autobiography, very little of

OPPOSITE: Tacitus' derisive comments about the female-led Sitones tribe reveal much about the extremely sexist Roman mindset.

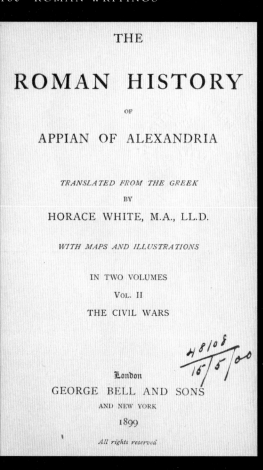

THE

ROMAN HISTORY

OF

APPIAN OF ALEXANDRIA

TRANSLATED FROM THE GREEK

BY

HORACE WHITE, M.A., LL.D.

WITH MAPS AND ILLUSTRATIONS

IN TWO VOLUMES

VOL. II

THE CIVIL WARS

London

GEORGE BELL AND SONS

AND NEW YORK

1899

ABOVE: Appian's *Roman History* is organised by theme rather than chronology. Only fragments remain of several of the books.

it survives, and some elements of his life are conjectured. He does seem to have been an important lawyer, and moved to Rome at some point in his career.

Appian wrote a large work entitled *Roman History*, which covers the entire history of the city, republic and empire from its mythical founding up to the campaigns of Emperor Trajan. Publication occurred before 162 CE, but the exact date is unclear. This work is unusual because it is arranged by theme rather than strict chronology. Thus all the conflicts with the Gauls are together despite occurring across a great span of time, as are the numerous civil wars of Rome.

Historians and scholars

Many Roman writers are not connected with mythology and religion to any great degree, if at all. They wrote on social and philosophical issues, created histories and biographies, and recorded their observations of the natural world. Some of these authors were also writing a form of present-day mythology when they praised the great deeds of their powerful patrons – or those whose patronage they hoped to receive. Unashamed flattery is not uncommon in the writing of the time, along with the usual connections back to the ancient Roman gods.

Given that a biography of an emperor who had been deified was the story of a god or how a man became one, biographers were writing in a curious genre that might be considered history-redefined-as-mythology. There are mythological elements at both ends of the tale – the founding-story and the connection of the emperor's bloodline back to the gods, and his final deification.

Some writers created their own myths, in the sense of relating real incidents in a way that suited their agenda. The most famous of these works is the account of the wars in Gaul fought by Julius Caesar. Written in the third person and presented as a factual account of the conflicts, these highly influential writings build the myth of Caesar as the all-conquering Roman hero – often at the expense of accuracy – and were of course the creation of their subject.

Caesar's account of his campaigns in Gaul conveniently skips over the occasions where he forced tribes into conflict in order to defeat them, increasing both his personal wealth and his reputation. Incidents that arose out of self-interest or that were in reality little more than politico-military showboating are presented as heroic battles to crush a threat to Rome. The outcome of these campaigns was to add large areas to Rome's territories and to present Caesar as the pre-eminent Roman hero.

In this case the victor quite literally wrote the history books, and presented his own version of what happened that reflected Caesar in the best possible light. *The Gallic Wars* is the definitive account of the events leading up to the civil wars that ultimately produced the Roman empire, yet much of it is self-myth created by Caesar. Although many details of his life and campaigns can be independently verified, other elements differ from the stories

BELOW: Julius Caesar receiving the surrender of the Gaulish chieftain Vercingetorix. In this case the victor quite literally wrote the history books.

of the gods only in that Jupiter did not sit down to write a self-glorifying memoir.

Unknown writers

The original author of some works may never be known, because they have been copied and their stories retold countless times by others. In some cases the originator of the story is also a myth. Such is the case with the *Orphic Hymns*. These poetic works recount elements of the *Orphic Mysteries*, which are claimed to have been first created by the mythical Orpheus. The Orphic myths present a different version of the relationships between

MYTHS AND MYTHOLOGY

The term 'myth' can be used in different contexts. It is normally used to refer to a story with a significant religious or paranormal element, but in fact originally simply meant 'account' or 'tale'. In the modern context, the term can be used to signify something widely believed but

untrue. Using that meaning of the word in Roman times would be hazardous, however, because the tales of the gods were an integral part of world history as well as religious practice.

Caesar's account of the Gallic Wars satisfies both definitions of the word 'myth'. It is a tale of questionable accuracy presented as true and believed to be so, at least in some quarters. It is also the story of how a man of divine descent became a god. Julius Caesar's family claimed descent from Julus, the son of Aeneas whose mother was the goddess Venus. Julius Caesar was the first Roman to be deified. Therefore his life story can be viewed as part of Roman mythology as well as a history of the times.

LEFT: **Julius Caesar was a pivotal figure in world history, yet many of the 'facts' known about his life and deeds are drawn from his own accounts of them, and therefore of questionable veracity.**

some of the gods, and contain stories that expand on or differ from those found elsewhere. In one such story, Orpheus ventured alive into the underworld to save his lover Eurydice. She had stepped on a viper and died, causing Orpheus tremendous grief, which he expressed through his mastery of the lyre.

Moved by Orpheus's music, the gods gave him leave to enter the underworld in pursuit of Eurydice. Depending on the version of the tale, Orpheus played for the gods of the underworld, who agreed to let Eurydice go; or Orpheus lulled the three-headed guardian hound Cerberus to sleep with his music, allowing the couple to make their escape.

Orpheus was undone at the entrance to the underworld. A condition on the departure of Eurydice was that Orpheus must walk ahead of her and not look back, but at the very threshold he turned to see she was safe. Eurydice was drawn back into the underworld and Orpheus had to leave without her. They were finally reunited after his death.

BELOW: **Orpheus plays for the gods of the underworld, seen through the imagination of Franz Franken in the early 1600s.**

5

THE MUNDANE & THE MYTHICAL WORLDS

Religion and mythology pervaded all aspects of daily life in ancient Rome. There were great festivals and smaller ones throughout the year, with family observances every day. Many of the temples also had an administrative or political role, and statues of the gods could be seen everywhere. Almost every act, place or object was associated with one or more of the gods.

Major religious festivals, known as feriae publicae, were held throughout the year. They took precedence over all normal activities, but although other business could not be conducted participation was not mandatory. The number of festivals scattered through the year might make it seem like nothing ever got done in ancient Rome, but these religious festivals were the only days off work for a Roman. Thus they acted as a sort of weekend and annual leave.

OPPOSITE: The adoption of Greek mythology placed all manner of mystical beasts – such as the Colchian Dragon slain by Jason – on the fringes of the Roman world.

Three types of public religious festival existed. Feriae stativae were observed on a specific date each year, whereas *feriae conceptivae* were assigned a suitable date. Feriae imperativae were held as necessary, typically to give thanks to the gods after a successful military campaign. A festival day could also be ordered if circumstances seemed to warrant it. A long drought or some other disaster might be seen as a reason for everyone to stop what they were doing and give glory to whichever gods might be able to help.

Major festivals of the year

The first festival of the year was dedicated to Janus and held on the first day of his month, marking the transition from one year to the next. This was followed by Compitalia, a celebration of the spirits associated with crossroads, which also marked the end of the agricultural year. Sementivae was observed three weeks later, on 24–26 January. This was dedicated to Tellus, and intended to bring about good conditions for sowing the new year's crops. Some observances continued for the next week or so, leading into the festival of Ceres on 2 February.

The first day of February was sacred to Juno, whose multiple aspects had associated holy days throughout the year. Juno was also one of the gods honoured at Lupercalia, on 15 February. As a fertility rite, Lupercalia also venerated the minor god Faunus. Unusually, the festival had its own group of specialized priests. Known as Luperci, these 'wolf-men' ran around the Palatine Hill armed with strips cut from the flesh of sacrificed goats and dogs. Any woman struck with these

BELOW: Festivals to Ceres, notably at the end of winter and in the spring, were intended to bring about a fertile growing season and ultimately a good harvest.

grisly trophies was said to be rendered fertile. It is likely that the wolf imagery referred back to the story of Romulus and Remus being suckled by a she-wolf.

The riotous fertility celebration of Lupercalia overlapped with the rather more sombre Parentalia, which honoured the dead. From 13 to 21 February, families paid respect to their own household's ancestors and recently deceased members. The culmination of this festival was known as Feralia, involving offerings at the graves of family members and a feast in their honour.

Later in the month, one of the two festivals named Equirria was held. This was in honour of Mars, and involved horse or chariot racing. A second Equirria took place in mid-March. Various reasons have been postulated for holding two similar festivals so close together. It may be that they were showcases of animal quality and rider skill intended to raise morale before the campaign season – in addition, of course, to obtaining the favour of Mars.

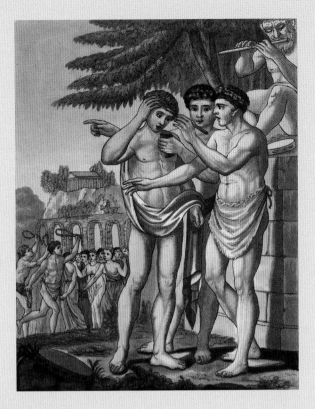

ABOVE: **The Lupercali specialised in a distinctly riotous form of religious observance, running around half-naked lashing women with strips of animal hide.**

Mid-March was an important time in the Roman calendar. The 14th was the date for the second Equirria and other festivals in honour of Mars, and the next day was dedicated to Anna Perenna. According to some Roman writers, this festival was accompanied by over-indulgence in alcohol and generally lewd behaviour.

The 17th of March was Liberalia, dedicated to Liber Pater – the 'free father' and protector of the plebian class. This was an extremely important occasion for a young man in ancient Rome, because it was the first occasion on which he would don the toga virilis. This was the clothing of an adult Roman male, marking the transition from boyhood to full status as a citizen. Further festivals honouring the war gods – Mars and Minerva – were undertaken from 19 to 23 March. Veneralia was held on 1 April, honouring Venus in the hope of success

ABOVE: Chariot racing was probably adopted from the Greeks. It became a part of religious festivals as well as a popular form of entertainment.

in love and marriage during the coming year. There were also broader connotations to the ceremonies. Faithfulness and good relations between the men and women of Rome contributed to the stability and success of the Roman state. Later in the month Cerialia was celebrated for eight days from the 12th to the 19th.

Cerialia was dedicated to Ceres, the goddess of grains. In part a solemn religious rite and in part an enormous and rather wild party, the festival was intended to protect the coming year's crops and ensure a good harvest. According to Ovid, part of the festivities included a 'fox race' in which the animals were released with burning torches attached to their tails. His explanation for this large-scale piece of animal cruelty is an old tale of how a boy tried to punish a fox for stealing chickens by setting it on fire, resulting in the frenzied animal racing all over his grain fields and burning them.

This seems a curious incident to recreate in a festival dedicated to grain, even if the aim is to symbolically punish all foxes for the destruction wrought in the original story. An alternative explanation is that the torches symbolized the one used by Ceres when she searched for her daughter Proserpina,

though how that connects to setting foxes on fire is a matter
for conjecture.

At the end of April, extending into the first days of May,
was Floralia. This celebrated the goddess Flora, associated with
flowers, and more generally the return of spring. The festival was
implemented around 240 BCE but ceased to be celebrated at some
point thereafter until 173 BCE. As usual, its reintroduction was
a pragmatic measure. A lingering winter and disruption to the
growing cycle were countered by the resumption of ceremonies
dedicated to Flora.

Mid-May saw a festival devoted to Mars Invictus on the 14th
and one devoted to Jupiter and Mercury the next day. Juno and
Mars were honoured on 1 June, with a festival devoted solely to
Jupiter Invictus on the 13th. In between was Vestalia, honouring
the goddess of the hearth and home. This was of importance to
millers and bakers as well as householders.

July began with a festival in honour of Juno, and from the
6th to the 13th games were held in honour of Apollo. These
started as a one-day event during the Second Punic War and
may have initially been intended as a temporary measure. Apollo
was apparently displeased about this, and plagues struck the city.

BELOW: There were no
'rest days' in Roman
society, but events
like the six days of
Floralia served a similar
function.

ABOVE: **The temple to Castor and Pollux was built in gratitude for victory at the Battle of Lake Regillus in 495 BCE.**

The games were reinstated to appease Apollo and expanded to a week-long festival.

In late July, Neptune was honoured with Neptunalia. His favour would ensure the summer was not too dry and sufficient water would be available for agriculture and domestic purposes. Even after Neptune was more strongly associated with the oceans rather than freshwater, his festival remained important even among people who never went near the sea.

August 13th was a day of celebration for multiple gods including Diana and Hercules, as well as various minor deities and spirits. Among them were Castor and Pollux, divine sons of Jupiter who were particularly popular with cavalrymen. Their part in the festivities was marked by a procession of cavalry led by two warriors on white horses representing the twins.

September began with the veneration of Jupiter and Juno, with the great festival of Jupiter Optimus Maximus running from the 5th to the 19th. Originally the festival was held on the 13th only and was dedicated to the Capitoline Trio. The day remained sacred to Juno and Minerva, whereas the festival of Jupiter spread out to fill two entire weeks. The event became known as the Great Games (or Roman Games) and involved chariot racing, exhibitions of horsemanship and all manner of other entertainments.

Another set of games dedicated to Jupiter took place on 15 October. Known as the Capitoline Games, this event was implemented in 387 BCE to celebrate the successful defence of the Capitoline Hill from invading Gauls. The Capitoline Games were eventually abandoned until 87 CE, when they were reinstated in a different form. This was on a four-year cycle and was a competitive event clearly inspired by the Greek Olympic Games. November saw the Plebian Games, running from the

4th to the 17th. Dedicated to Jupiter, the games celebrated the achievements of the ordinary people of Rome, rather than the great leaders and statesmen. The final major festival of the calendar year was Saturnalia, originally a single day but eventually taking place from the 17th to the 23rd December. The festival was associated with the winter solstice, which fell on 25 December in the Roman calendar.

Saturnalia was dedicated to Saturn, who despite being overthrown as ruler of the universe remained important as a god of agriculture and thus food supply. Saturnalia was a time of peace and goodwill, characterized by many practices that are still familiar today. Feasting, gift-giving and merriment were encouraged, and slaves were treated as free equals for the day.

The practice of appointing a Saturnalicius princeps in each household to oversee the festivities was carried on in European society with the designation of a 'lord of misrule' at some celebrations. This might be a risky position at a king's

BELOW: The winter feast of Saturnalia was a time of peace and goodwill. Its influence on the later festival of Christmas is obvious.

court, where the lord of misrule had to create as much cheeky fun as possible without generating resentment to be acted on after the festival. The Saturnalicius princeps in an ordinary household might not be in much danger, but those hosting parties for the rich and powerful would need to be mindful of politics and personalities.

Mythological give and take

The relationship between Romans and their gods – and other supernatural beings – was pragmatic, based either on the concept of worship in return for assistance or propitiation to avoid misfortune. Propitiating the right spirit was every bit as important as sharpening tools or loading a farm wagon correctly. Indeed, no matter how well-maintained and carefully loaded the wagon might be, it could still lose a wheel or have its load inexplicably topple if an offended local spirit took a dislike to it.

AN ANCESTOR WHO HAD GREATLY BENEFITED THE FAMILY MIGHT EXPECT TO BE VENERATED FOR IT FOREVER.

The need to propitiate such a huge variety of spirits and deities ensured there were many festivals and celebrations throughout the year in addition to those dedicated to the major gods. Some were rather niche and others widespread but of relatively low importance. Some festivals were not annual, such as the Taurian Games, which were held in late June every fifth year. This was in honour of the gods of the underworld, and intended to avert their wrath.

Other events took place at multiple times of the year. The Ides – the 13th or 15th depending on the month – were sacred to Jupiter, whatever else was happening at the time. Three times in the year the Lapis Manalis, or 'stone of the underworld', would be removed from its position atop the sacred pit believed to give access to the underworld. This would allow the spirits of the departed and the old gods to join in the festivities and prevent them from becoming hostile. The opening of the Mundus, the sacred pit, took place on 24 August, 5 October and 8 November.

In addition, each household would observe its own religious ceremonies – feriae privatae – whenever necessary. This might mean honouring a notable ancestor or observing a period of mourning and cleansing after the death of a family member.

This was an important observation because it ensured the dead and the living were kept separate; until the prescribed 10-day mourning period was complete the family of the deceased might be a link back to the world of the living where the restless soul could cause trouble.

Some festivals were religious in nature but not directed specifically at any one god. Among these was the Supplicia Canum, possibly held in August. The ceremony originated from an incident in 390 BCE, when the Gauls attempted a sneak attack at night and fed the hungry dogs to prevent them from barking an alarm.

The gambit worked, but the alarm was raised by geese and the attack was driven off. Thereafter, dogs were punished at the Supplicia Canum festival. Some sources state they were crucified on crosses; others say a Y-shaped fork arrangement was used. Meanwhile, geese were praised and lauded.

BELOW: Sacred geese depicted at the temple of Juno, on the Capitoline Hill where they raised a timely alarm.

Even if this had been done just once it might seem extremely vindictive, but to repeat the process every year requires some explanation. The Romans considered everything that happened to be of mythological or religious significance, so punishing dogs for failing to raise the alarm might ensure they did their jobs properly. On the other hand, failing to recognize the great service done by the geese could result in assistance being withheld – by geese or perhaps some other unexpected benefactor – in the future. Additionally, geese were sacred to Juno. Honouring them would probably please her, which was always wise.

Private religious events reflected the same need to keep the relevant gods and spirits happy. An ancestor who had greatly benefited the family might expect to be venerated for it forever. Failing to recognize their achievements might bring misfortune. A Roman citizen who properly honoured the ancestors could expect to receive the same in their time; one who disrespected notable forebears would wisely fear being forgotten.

Omens and auguries

Omens were extremely important to Romans of all social levels. Any out-of-the-ordinary event could be considered an omen – unseasonable storms, the birth of a deformed animal, freak accidents or random pieces of good fortune could all be interpreted as omens. Any person who observed what they thought was an omen could report it, after which it would be interpreted by experts.

Specialists at interpreting omens were known as haruspices. The practice was inherited from the Etruscans but was continued into imperial times. Haruspices were trained in their art and followed a well-established set of rules. In addition to interpreting whatever omens were naturally occurring, they also consulted the entrails of sacrificed animals to make specific determinations.

The almost scientific practice of the haruspices contrasted with the far less formal divinations found in native Roman culture. The word 'divination' has taken on a wider meaning

RIGHT: Interpreting the entrails of sacrificed animals was a precise and almost scientific skill requiring lengthy training.

since Roman times, and is today used to describe a wide range of attempts to determine the future. In the Roman context divination was an attempt to discern the will of the gods. This would allow predictions to be made – an action that was acceptable to the gods or aligned with their intentions would succeed, whereas challenging the will of the gods was a sure route to disaster. However, Roman divination did not seek to determine exactly what was to come – it was guidance, rather than predication.

Supernatural guidance was available to those who could journey to an oracle. When the state was in need of guidance the oracle at Delphi, sacred to Apollo, would be consulted. Another source of advice was the Sibylline Books, stored in the Temple of Jupiter on the Capitoline Hill. These writings were not intended for nor available to common Romans. The prophecies were about the Roman state as a whole and were used in times of great crisis.

The Sibylline Books were destroyed in 82 BCE, when fire consumed the temple. They were sufficiently important to the well-being of the state that great effort was made to replace them. All the books of prophecy that could be found were collected from the citizens of Rome and ambassadors sought out any that could be found in other cities. Many of the books thus collected were considered to be fake or inaccurate, and were burned. The remainder were placed in the rebuilt temple of Jupiter and private citizens were banned from owning such books in the future.

One of the primary means of divination was augury; observing the behaviour of birds to determine the omens. This could be done by watching wild birds, but there were circumstances in which this might not be possible. One example was aboard a vessel about to sail into battle on the open sea. Waiting for birds that might or might not make an appearance was impractical,

ABOVE: Tarquinius Superbus eventually bought three of the original nine books of prophecy from the Sybil. Those failing to find appropriate guidance within might have lamented his failure to obtain the full set.

ANCIENT CONSPIRACY THEORISTS?

It is easy to imagine the reaction of some Romans to the ban on private ownership of books of prophecy. What were the authorities trying to conceal? What right did they have to deprive Roman citizens of divine guidance? This might in part explain the popularity of 'mystery cults' such as those of Bacchus, Isis and Orpheus. All of them promised to reveal secrets to those rising high enough in their ranks. Some such cults will no doubt have been scams intended to make money from seekers of divine knowledge, or bizarre concoctions resembling a mythological conspiracy theory. Others will have been sincere though not necessarily correct in their beliefs – if such a thing is possible at all. The lure of cosmic secrets will have drawn adherents to all of these mystery cults in the same manner we see on the internet today.

BELOW: **The 'mystery cult' of Isis did not achieve the popularity of Bacchus or Mithras, but nevertheless had adherents right across the empire.**

and the Romans were a practical people. Therefore, caged chickens were brought along for the purpose of augury. Once they were released, the chickens were fed. If they ate heartily, the omens were good. If they refused food or escaped, the situation was deemed unfavourable.

The position of augur was prestigious and lucrative, and could give the holder great influence. Originally open only to the patrician class, from about 300 BCE the post was available to plebians. It was not always possible to agree on the interpretation of an augury, and augurs had a tendency to be rather vague. Nevertheless they were consulted in all major matters, including lawsuits, and were no doubt subject to a great deal of political pressure.

According to legend, Romulus and Remus agreed to consult an augur to determine whose location for their proposed city best pleased the gods. The brothers argued about whose omens were more favourable – was it better to have seen more birds, or to have seen them first? Eventually the matter was settled by violence.

ABOVE: The importance of divination was such that some political and legal decisions came down to which faction had the best augurs rather than arguments about law and necessity.

The physical and supernatural world

The Romans were highly organized and offered a good education to their citizens. Information was stored and disseminated as required or desired. In short, they knew a great deal about their world and had good maps of the places they had visited. At the same time, accounts of some distant places are tinged with supernatural fear. There are mentions of distant lands populated by strange half-human creatures and unnerving natural conditions at the edges of the known world.

Tacitus speculates that there may be another set of Pillars of Hercules in the far north, though there are no legends of Hercules ever venturing beyond the Mediterranean region. He may have been referring to a physical phenomenon, a narrow and high-bounded strait leading to another ocean, rather than a place of supernatural origin. However, it was widely believed that such places existed. Roman mythology held that there were minor deities associated with many geographical features or areas of the countryside. Fauns and nymphs might be encountered or angered by an unwary traveller, and there was always the possibility of problems on the road resulting from inadequate propitiation of local spirits. There were also places with supernatural significance, some of them quite close to home territory.

Mount Etna, located in eastern Sicily, has been active throughout history. In addition to its physical significance, Etna was home to Vulcan, the forge god, and was where he manufactured magical treasures for the other gods. It would be easy to imagine the smoke and rumblings – and occasional eruptions – resulted from the work of a god.

Another volcanic area of mythological significance was Lake Avernus, which lay in the caldera of an extinct volcano. It was first discovered by Greeks, who settled nearby and built the town of Cumae. Although the volcano was no longer active, the region had numerous hot springs and vents that released sulphurous gases. Not surprisingly, the ancient Greeks thought this might be the entrance to the underworld, and when the Romans incorporated the region into their territory the belief persisted.

BELOW: The fires of Mount Etna, site of Vulcan's forge, were a constant reminder of the presence of gods in the mortal world.

Lake Avernus is mentioned in Virgil as the point of entry used by Aeneas in his journey to the underworld. There is also a reference in Homer's *Odyssey* to such a place, though Homer is vague about the location. In the *Aeneid*, Aeneas is guided by the Sibyl, who dwells in a cave nearby and issues prophecies containing the wisdom of Apollo.

Although the Cumaean Sybil and others like her

were important as sources of prophecy and oracular advice, the most famous oracle was at Delphi. According to legend, Apollo and Diana slew a great monster that had been sent to harass their mother, causing it to fall into a fissure in the ground near Delphi. Henceforth, foul fumes issued from the fissure, which would cause anyone breathing them to enter a trance-like state. It was believed that Apollo spoke to them during their madness, imparting wisdom that could be passed to others.

Eventually, a priestess was appointed to serve as the oracle. Known as the Pythea, she acted as a conduit between visitors to the shrine and Apollo himself. Many of those coming to the Pythea with questions were representatives of the state or powerful individuals, and thus the oracle played an important role in shaping the course of Roman history. Over the centuries many women served as the Pythea, and at times multiple priestesses were needed to deal with the volume of information being requested.

Dangerous locations also existed close to home. The tale of Ulysses, Romanized from the Greek Odyssey, told of a dangerous and narrow passage, which was later identified as the Strait of Messina. This lies between the toe of Italy and nearby Sicily. It is not clear whether 'modern' Romans actually believed the dangers

ABOVE: The Temple of Apollo at Lake Avernus, whose name means 'birdless'. This was probably due to toxic fumes killing or driving off local wildlife.

still existed, but this was a seaway they would have to use on a regular basis. According to Odyssia, expanded on by Ovid, one of the dangers of the strait was a monster named Scylla, who had once been human. Transformed by the sorceress Circe, Scylla had 12 feet and six heads on long necks, with which she reached out to snatch sailors from passing ships. Scylla had positioned herself to take advantage of another hazard on the other side of the strait. This was Charybdis, who could drink the waters nearby and swallow ships. Charybdis was essentially a personification of a dangerous whirlpool, and when ships steered close to the opposite shore to avoid it, Scylla fed on their crews.

Roman writings make little mention of where the other gods lived. Some sources refer to Mount Olympus in Greece, which is plausible given that many of the major Roman gods were also known by their former Greek names. Since their stories were in many cases co-opted wholesale it follows that their home was

not shifted. This is not the case for all the major gods, however. Neptune was thought to dwell under the sea in some place inaccessible to mortals, and the gods of the underworld had a palace at the entrance to the Elysian Fields.

It remains unclear where the average Roman drew the line between physical and supernatural worlds. If the gods existed and the dead had to be honoured to prevent them interfering in the affairs of mortals, it was not much of a stretch to fear an encounter with a mythological being or spirit, and indeed this was an explanation for unexpected good or bad fortune. Individuals were willing to consult books of prophecy or travel to an oracle, so perhaps they also believed they might stray into the path of a mythical monster if they were not careful. The accepted presence of any mythical elements within daily life opened the door for acceptance of all of them.

Constellations and star signs

The planets and constellations played a part in Roman mythology, representing various creatures and beings, and the Romans also inherited the practice of astrology from the Greeks. It seems to have developed in Mesopotamia and spread westward into Greece. Initially a fairly simple reading of omens associated with events in the sky, over time the practice developed into a recognizable ancestor of modern astrology.

It is known that the death of Alexander the Great in Babylon was predicted by astrology, and in the years that followed his successors appointed their own astrologers. Inevitably the practice was adopted by the Romans, though not entirely without opposition. By the time the republic had become an empire, predictions based on a horoscope were considered accurate enough to base political decisions on. The emperor Tiberius ordered the execution of several notable individuals based on horoscopes that suggested they might be a threat to him.

The constellations known by ancient Romans are recognizable today, and they used similar star signs in their horoscopes. The emperor Augustus, for example, was a Capricorn and used the goat that symbolized on coins minted in his name. Many of the Roman constellations were connected with mythological figures

IT IS KNOWN THAT THE DEATH OF ALEXANDER THE GREAT IN BABYLON WAS PREDICTED BY ASTROLOGY, AND IN THE YEARS THAT FOLLOWED HIS SUCCESSORS APPOINTED THEIR OWN ASTROLOGERS.

or tales. The Roman statesman Cicero, famous for defending the ideals of the republic and resisting the transition to empire, translated a Greek poem that became known as the Aratea after its original writer, Aratus. The subject of this poem was the constellations as the Greeks knew them. Some of these constellations are connected by their mythical stories, such as Aquarius and Aquila.

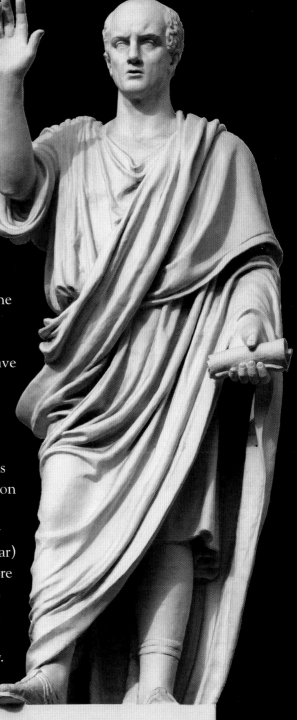

A mortal named Ganymede became the constellation Aquarius – the water bearer – after being carried off by Jupiter's eagle Aquila. Ganymede was a prince of Troy who was thought by the gods to be the most handsome man they had ever seen. This conflicts with the tale of Adonis, who was also given this distinction. Perhaps the gods had different tastes in men – Adonis was the lover of Venus and was tragically killed by wild animals that were immune to his charms, whereas Ganymede was taken from the mortal world to serve Jupiter.

Jupiter is normally said to have sent his eagle Aquila to fetch Ganymede, but may have gone himself. He was fond of transforming himself into other creatures, and might have impersonated his eagle to avoid the suspicion of Juno. Either way, Ganymede was brought to the court of Jupiter to serve as a cup-bearer and honoured as the constellation of Aquarius.

Some constellations represented objects or items from mythological stories. Ara (the Altar) represented an altar upon which the gods swore allegiance to one another before they went to battle with Saturn for control of the universe. This event, and the battle that followed, are given greater importance in Greek mythology.

ABOVE: The tale of Ganymede is typical of Roman mythology. The gods got what they wanted because they had the power to make it happen, and mortals were expected to bow to their will.

It is notable that although many constellations were the same as those recognized by the Greeks but with Roman names, Ara is unchanged from the Greek. On the other hand Libra, the scales, represents a different interpretation from that used by the Greeks. They considered this group to be the claws of Scorpio, whereas the Roman interpretation persists to this day. Libra was a favourable sign to the ancient Romans, representing justice.

Other constellations represent characters – some of them quite minor – from Roman mythology. Cancer represents the ill-fated giant crab sent by Juno to impede Hercules in his fight with the Lernaean Hydra. The crab was able to slow Hercules down by grabbing his foot with its pincers, but was unceremoniously stomped to death. Its doomed valour was rewarded by a place in the sky. Likewise, Delphinus represents

the brave dolphin that ventured out into the Atlantic Ocean in search of the nymph Salacia and convinced her to become the wife of Neptune.

The constellation of Boötes is generally considered to represent Arcas, a son of Zeus and Callisto. Callisto was either a mortal princess or a nymph, depending on the source. In the latter version of the tale, she was one of the companions of Diana. This group of nymphs was famed for their chastity, but Callisto was seduced by Jupiter and turned into a bear. In some variants this was done by Jupiter to avoid the anger of Juno; in others Diana or Juno performs the transformation. Callisto was then slain by Diana, possibly by mistake, and was placed in the sky as the constellation Ursa Major. According to Ovid, Arcas became the star Arcturus.

In another version of the tale Callisto is a mortal, daughter of King Lycaon of Arcadia. The king decides, rather unwisely, to test the omniscience of Jupiter by mixing the child's flesh into a meal and having it served to the god. Jupiter, understandably perhaps, responds with a volley of thunderbolts, which kill Lycaon's sons, before bringing his own child Arcas back to life. The king himself is transformed into a wolf. Juno then turns Callisto into a bear as punishment for being the object of Jupiter's affections. When an adult Arcas begins to hunt the bear, not knowing it is his mother, Jupiter saves them both from tragedy by making them into constellations.

BELOW: An alternate version of the origins of Delphinus has Apollo create the constellation to reward dolphins for saving the life of the poet Arion.

RIGHT: Transformed into a bear, Callisto was about to be slain by her own son Arcas. Both were saved by Jupiter's intervention.

OPPOSITE: The poem 'Aratea' was translated by Cicero. Thus the Greek constellations were popularised in the Roman world.

The constellation of Auriga, also known as the Charioteer, is sometimes said to represent the child of Minerva and Vulcan. Despite having manoeuvred Venus into becoming his wife, Vulcan was displeased with their loveless marriage and began to desire Minerva. He attempted to force himself on the chaste goddess of war, which was obviously a doomed enterprise. Defeated, all Vulcan succeeded in doing was splashing some of his semen on Minerva's leg. She wiped it off and threw away the cloth, which fell on the ground. From this unpromising beginning was born Auriga, who was lame like his father and made use of a chariot for transport.

Sagittarius represents the noble Cheiron, tutor of heroes and learned centaur of culture. Accidentally shot with a poisoned arrow by Hercules, Cheiron's knowledge of medicine was insufficient to cure himself but, being immortal, he could not escape the pain of the poison. Cheiron found escape by volunteering to replace Prometheus, who was chained to a rock to be eternally tormented by vultures as punishment for giving the secret of fire to mortals. This permitted Cheiron to relinquish his immortality and ended the suffering of Prometheus. The wise centaur was granted a place in the heavens by Jupiter in honour of this deed. The constellation of Centaurus is sometimes considered to represent Cheiron, but more commonly is associated with the centaur race as a whole.

Sinumeros medio in cielo centaurus habebit.
Ipse que cerulea contectus nube feretur.
Atque arma tenui caligine seserigiet umbra
At signorum obitu uiret metuenda fauoni.
Ille autem centaurus in alta sede locatus
Qua sese clare conlucent scorpios infert.
Hae subter partem perpotans ipse uirilem
Cedit qui partis properat coniungere chelis.
Hic dextram porgens quadriper quia tenetur
Quam nemo certo donauit nomine gratum
Tendit et inlustrem truculentus cedit ad aram

:CENTAVR

Some constellations are related. The great hunter Orion attracted the ire of Juno by announcing his intention to kill all of the animals in the whole world, so she sent the giant scorpion represented by Scorpio to deal with him. Both were placed in the sky as a reminder of the tale, which is commonly held to be a warning to respect the natural word. It is also possible that the constellations of Orion and Scorpio are reminders that mortals should know their limits. Similarly, the constellations of Hercules and Leo may be related, given that Leo can be taken to represent one of the lions battled by the hero.

The legend of Perseus

The tale of Perseus is connected with several Roman constellations. It passed more or less unchanged from Greek to Roman mythology, though the names of some participants were Romanized. Perseus was a demigod fathered by Jupiter on Danae, a princess of Argos. Danae and Perseus were locked in a chest and hurled into the sea by Danae's father, who had been warned he would be slain by his grandson. They washed up on the island of Seriphus, whose king took a liking to Danae.

BELOW: **Perseus, a Greek hero co-opted wholesale by the Romans, is most famous for slaying the Gorgon Medusa.**

Wanting Danae's son out of the way, King Polydectes of Seriphus set Perseus the task of bringing him the head of Medusa, one of the three monstrous Gorgons. To accomplish this impossible task Perseus extorted magical treasures from the Graeae, magical hags who possessed a single eye and one tooth between them. Since Medusa's direct gaze could turn anyone to stone, Perseus used his brightly reflective shield as a mirror to locate his target and decapitated her with a magical sword. The head was placed in a bag, at which point Perseus could begin his journey home. This was greatly assisted by the use of winged sandals that allowed the wearer to fly.

Perseus returned home and tricked king Polydectes into opening the bag

containing Medusa's head. However, before this he became involved in an incident that produced several constellations, including Cassiopeia and Andromeda.

According to legend, Cassiopeia was a queen of Ethiopia and wife to King Cepheus. Cassiopeia boasted that her daughter Andromeda was the most beautiful being in existence, which naturally angered the gods. Neptune sent a great monster named Cetus, generally identified as a whale, to harass the coastline. To appease the creature, Andromeda was chained to a rock as a sacrifice. She was rescued by Perseus, who was returning from slaying Medusa and used her severed head as a weapon. Even in death, Medusa's gaze could turn anyone to stone, and Cetus was no exception.

Despite the rescue of the sacrifice and the slaying of their monster, the gods were appeased. Perhaps they approved of

ABOVE: Although the tale of Perseus has him using the head of Medusa to turn Cetus to stone, he is depicted here battling the monster by more physical means.

the valour shown by Perseus, but for whatever reason there were no further consequences for the people of Ethiopia. Andromeda married Perseus and ultimately was placed in the sky as a constellation. Cassiopeia, too, became a constellation but apparently as a punishment rather than an honour. She was bound to a chair, which was set to whirl around Polaris, the Pole Star, for all eternity. King Cepheus was honoured by being made a constellation without any uncomfortable circumstances, as was the monster Cetus.

A lost constellation

Many constellations have retained their Roman names and identities into modern times, but one that has not is Argo Navis. This once represented the ship used by Jason and the Argonauts in their voyage to obtain the golden fleece. Although participants in the voyage – including Hercules, Castor and Pollux (as Gemini) – have been immortalized among the constellations, the vessel herself has not.

JASON WAS BORN IN SECRET AND SENT AWAY TO BE PROTECTED AND TUTORED BY THE CENTAUR CHEIRON.

Jason's family situation is typically convoluted. His father was Aeson, son of king Cretheus of Iolcus, making him the rightful heir to the throne. However, Aeson had a half-brother named Pelias who was fathered by Neptune. Pelias overthrew Cretheus and imprisoned him, murdering his relatives to protect the succession for Pelias's own line. Jason was born in secret and sent away to be protected and tutored by the centaur Cheiron.

When he was old enough, Jason set out to reclaim his kingdom. Along the way he helped an old woman cross a stream, not realizing it was Juno in disguise. Pelias had angered the goddess by murdering his stepmother in Juno's own temple, and she decided to take revenge on him by way of Jason. However, Pelias had been warned by the oracle at Delphi to beware of a man with one sandal, and since Jason had lost one of his in the stream he was identified as a threat.

Pelias met Jason and offered him the throne, on one condition. Jason had to retrieve the legendary golden fleece and bring it back to Iolcus. He agreed, despite the fact this was a near-impossible task, and began making his preparations. This required building a mighty ship and assembling a crew of heroes to sail it.

Jason's crew included many notable individuals. Hercules was among them, as were the twins Castor and Pollux. The great musician Orpheus also joined the crew, who were known as Argonauts after their ship, *Argo*. They had many adventures, beginning with an incident on the island of Lemnos. The women of the island had been cursed with tremendous body odour by Venus, as punishment for failing to worship her properly. Rejected by their menfolk, the women of Lemnos murdered them. For whatever reason Jason and his crew were not put off

ARIES AND THE GOLDEN FLEECE

The golden fleece had once belonged to a magical winged ram named Aries, who rescued the children of King Athamas of Orchomenus. Named Phrixos and Helle, the children were semi-divine because their mother was the cloud nymph Nubes. They were hated by King Athamas's second wife, Ino, who arranged for them to be sacrificed. Aries flew down and rescued the children, attempting to carry them to safety in a far-off land. Helle was unable to cling on for the whole journey, and fell into the sea, where she died. The area is known as the Hellespont in her memory.

Phrixos survived the journey and was delivered to King Aeetes of Colchis. At first this went well for Phrixos; he married the king's daughter. Aries fared rather more poorly; Phrixos sacrificed him to the gods and gave his golden fleece to King Aeetes. Soon after, Aeetes learned of a prophecy that a member of his family would betray him and his kingdom would be lost to a stranger who came to take the fleece. Apparently forgetting that Phrixos had gifted him the magical fleece, Aeetes killed his son-in-law and set magical creatures to guard the fleece. In honour of his sacrifice, Aries was set in the heavens as a constellation.

by the smell of the women and lingered on Lemnos for some time. Eventually resuming their journey the Argonauts passed through the Hellespont, where they encountered the hospitable but unaccountably forgetful King Cyzicus. While most of the Argonauts were away from their ship foraging for provisions, the vessel was attacked by six-armed monsters the king had for some reason neglected to mention.

Hercules was instrumental in defending the ship and her crew, and the monsters were eventually defeated. Sailing away in a hurry, the Argonauts got lost at night and ended up back where they had started. There they encountered King Cyzicus but failed to recognize him in the darkness. The heroes inflicted great losses on Cyzicus's followers and slew him before they realized their mistake. After attending the funeral of the unfortunate Cyzicus, the Argonauts sailed on until Hercules broke his oar. Venturing ashore to find wood for a replacement, Hercules was accompanied by his friend Hylas. Hylas was bewitched by a water-nymph and drowned, and in great sorrow Hercules left the expedition. Pollux, a great boxer, dealt with the next obstacle. This was King Amycus of the Bebryces tribe, who liked to fight everyone he met. Pollux won the fight but the Argonauts were then attacked by the vengeful Bebryces.

Next the Argonauts encountered Phineus, an old man who had been cursed by Jupiter. His prophecies and visions revealed more than Jupiter liked, so he was harassed by winged creatures named Harpies whenever he sat down to a meal. The Argonauts made a plan to kill the Harpies, but instead struck a bargain with the goddess Arcus (Iris in the Greek version), who was their sister. In return for their lives the Harpies agreed to leave Phineus alone. The grateful Phineus told Jason how to safely pass the gigantic rocks known as the Cyanae Insulae (Symplegades in the Greek version), which smashed together to crush unwary ships. A dove released by Jason got through for the loss of a tail feather; *Argo* followed at great speed and suffered only slight damage to her stern.

After the passage of the *Argo*, the great rocks ceased to crush ships, and more immediately the Argonauts entered the Black Sea. They were aided by Jupiter, whose winds blew them away from the lands of the Amazons, who would have been tough enemies, but soon afterwards the ship was attacked by monstrous birds. These were the survivors of the Stymphalian birds, recently driven from their home by Hercules

BELOW: **The Argonauts rescued Phineus from the Harpies by diplomacy – albeit backed by the threat of force – rather than the usual application of heroic violence.**

as part of his labours. The Argonauts frightened the birds off by making a great deal of noise. Soon afterwards, the ship arrived in Colchis and Jason fell almost immediately in love with Medea, daughter of King Aeetes. This was the doing of Juno, by way of instructions to Venus, who in turn sent Cupid to shoot both with love-arrows. Jason was rather too candid about his intentions, telling Aeetes he planned to take the golden fleece. Aeetes agreed to relinquish the fleece if Jason could tame the fire-breathing bulls that guarded it.

With magical help from Medea, Jason succeeded in controlling the bulls. The sleepless dragon that also guarded the

BELOW: A 1745 depiction of Jason and Medea in the Temple of Jupiter, by Jean Francois de Troy.

fleece was lulled into slumber by Orpheus, enabling Jason to take the fleece. Rather than keep his promise Aeetes naturally plotted to kill the Argonauts, but they suspected treachery and were already heading for their ship. Aeetes and his son Apsyrtus pursued Jason and his crew, but gave up when Apsyrtus was slain.

Despite previously helping Jason, Jupiter answered the prayers of Aeetes for vengeance. He drove *Argo* off course with a mighty wind, sending the ship to the island where the sorceress Circe lived. She did not turn the crew into pigs, as she had done to the companions of Ulysses, but she sent them away when she learned of the death of Apsyrtus, who was her nephew.

The Argonauts then encountered the Sirens, whose songs would lure sailors to their death on the rocks where the Sirens sat. Whereas Ulysses' men had blocked up their ears with wax, the Argonauts were protected by the music of Orpheus. The Sirens were unable to compete with the greatest of all mortal musicians, and the Argonauts escaped.

Evading the twin threats of the monster Scylla and the whirlpool Charybdis, the Argonauts then had to contend with a bronze giant named Talos, who could only be slain by way of a vein at the back of his ankle. This was accomplished by Medea's magic, and thereafter the Argonauts created the island of Santorini. One of

WHEREAS ULYSSES' MEN HAD BLOCKED UP THEIR EARS WITH WAX, THE ARGONAUTS WERE PROTECTED BY THE MUSIC OF ORPHEUS.

ABOVE: **Gaining the Golden Fleece was the high point of Jason's career. Ultimately he was a tool for the gods, to be cast aside and forgotten when he was no longer of use.**

them had dreamed he had sex with a sea nymph who was fearful of what her father Neptune might do if he found out she was pregnant. The sailor was advised to throw overboard a clod of earth he carried with him. This grew into the island, creating a safe home where the nymph would raise their children.

Finally the Argonauts reached Iolcus and presented the golden fleece to Pelias, expecting him to keep his word and hand over the kingdom. He had no intention of doing so, and had already murdered the captive Aeson. Instead of merely killing Pelias, Jason asked Medea to help him take grisly revenge for the death of his father. Tricked into believing Medea could restore their father's youth, Pelias's daughters cut him into pieces and boiled them.

Having won his kingdom, Jason could not keep it. The people of Iolcus were unwilling to accept the sorceress Medea as their queen, so Jason abdicated and went to live quietly in Corinth.

He was simply cast aside by Juno, who had engineered the whole adventure to put Medea in a position to kill Pelias. Once the deed was done, Juno had no use for her pawns.

Jason met an anticlimactic end. Realizing he had become attracted to a Corinthian princess, Medea killed her. She also murdered the three children she had borne with Jason before abandoning him and moving to Athens. Jason lingered in obscurity until he could stand it no more. He begged Jupiter for an ending and, as he sat beside the decaying hulk of *Argo*, a piece broke off.

Jason was killed by a fragment of his own great ship, passing from heroic glory into obscurity. He was not rewarded with a place among the constellations but his tale remained important to Greek and later Roman mythology. So many elements and personalities were intertwined – Hercules, Castor and Pollux, Orpheus, Scylla and Charybdis and the Amazons to name but a few – that Jason's tale became an essential part of Mediterranean mythology.

BELOW: Creusa was the wife of Aeneas, lost during the escape from Troy. Later in the *Aeneid* she appears to Aeneas and presents him with a great deal of information.

6

THE LEGACY OF ROMAN MYTHOLOGY

Roman mythology left a powerful legacy all across Europe and even beyond. Although the power of the western Roman empire was broken and the last emperor deposed in 476 CE, the city itself retained enormous significance as a symbol if not a seat of power. Latin remained a common language permitting communication between disparate peoples, and concepts could be easily transmitted using Roman idiom and cultural references.

The period after the fall of Rome was for a long time described as a 'dark age', in which the 'light of Rome' was extinguished and Europe fell into violent chaos. It is true that this was a time of great turbulence but it might better be described as an era in which the torch was passed to a new generation of active young cultures.

OPPOSITE: Mythology is, by its very nature, mutable. This 1736 depiction of the Apotheosis of Hercules is very different from the way the ancient Romans might have imagined the event.

There was no single reason for the collapse of the Roman empire, nor was it a catastrophic or sudden event. The empire had become too large to govern effectively, and even splitting it into eastern and western segments could not restore the level of organization required to operate such a gigantic state. Plagues had weakened the empire at a time when new threats required large reserves of manpower. Lack of unity was another problem – money and lives were spent in civil wars instead of securing the borders.

Perhaps Rome might have weathered all these troubles, had its attention and energy been directed at preserving the empire. Instead, external events were typically viewed in terms of their importance to local politics. It is unlikely that the politicians of late Rome were able to envisage the 'big picture' – it was simply too big. Nor could they take direct action against distant problems – not when they had to fend off the schemes of their rivals. Where the threat of barbarian invasion was once the impetus for sweeping social and military reforms, the later empire must have seemed eternal. A defeat on the distant borders was not a threat to the survival of Rome, but it was an opportunity to bring down a rival who might be implicated and thus discredited.

With attention turned inward and resources increasingly limited, the outer Roman provinces came under immense pressure from migrating 'barbarian' peoples. The primary reason for this was the arrival in eastern Europe of the Huns, whose presence drove whole confederations of tribes to move westwards seeking new and safe lands. This caused conflict with Romanized peoples, a problem partially solved by

BELOW: The defeat of the Huns at the Catalaunian Fields owed at least as much to the emerging Frankish culture as to the power of the Roman Empire.

allowing some of the new arrivals to settle within the borders of the empire as foederati. Essentially these groups were given a place to live in return for defending the frontiers against the next wave of migrants and the Huns themselves.

The Hunnish invasion was eventually halted in what is now France. The army responsible for their final defeat at the battle of the Catalaunian Fields was a joint Roman–Frankish force rather than a Roman army with non-Roman allies or auxiliary troops. The Franks were well on their way to becoming an independent state, even though their land was still officially Roman territory. So it was elsewhere, as the displaced tribes settled where they could and carved out their own kingdoms.

Even after the fall of the western Roman empire, Roman customs and language enabled communication and trade between the peoples of Europe. The literate classes still wrote in Latin and civilized people sometimes referred to themselves as Romans. The new kingdoms of Europe went their own way, gradually moving away from Roman culture as their own developed. Yet this common ancestry continued to manifest in place names, figures of speech and the occasional Latin phrase used by those wishing to demonstrate a high level of education.

ABOVE: The *Historia Brittonum* was long supposed to be factual, but has been established as mostly fiction or myth. It contains the earliest known appearance of the figure eventually known as King Arthur.

Co-opted history

The mythology of ancient Rome leads, by a convoluted path, to the mythical history of Britain and the legend of King Arthur. Writing around 1136 CE, Geoffrey of Monmouth created a great work of literature entitled *Historia Regum Britanniae* – History of the Kings of Britain. This is in fact a pseudohistory, with significant parts appearing to be simply made up. It draws on another great work of the times, the *Historia Brittonum*. This is generally credited to the monk Nennius and may date from around AD 800–830. It contains the first references to the character who would evolve into the legendary King Arthur. According to these works of pseudohistory, the family of

Aeneas settled in Italy and played their part in the founding of Rome. Aeneas's great-grandson, named Brutus, was exiled for accidentally killing his father so continued the family tradition of wandering around doing great deeds. After founding the city of Troyes he moved on, eventually arriving on the island of Albion around 1100 BCE.

Brutus conquered all of Albion and founded a city named Troia Nova as his capital. The name of the city became corrupted to Trinovantum and was later changed to London. Among his descendants were Eburacus, who according to this account built Edinburgh Castle long before Rome was founded. Another was a man named Leir, the basis for Shakespeare's play King Lear. Shakespeare's version is rather more gloomy than the account featured in Geoffrey of Monmouth's *Historia Regum Brittaniae*.

BELOW: Geoffrey of Monmouth is generally credited with creating the 'King Arthur Myth' which pervades much of British literature and popular culture.

After a period of relative stability, a succession dispute led to war between Belinus and Brennius, sons of the king of the Britons. Brennius went to Gaul and became a king of the Allobroges tribe, who helped him regain his lands. The brothers then conquered Gaul and forced a treaty on Rome. This was not honoured, so the brothers conquered Rome. Brennius remained there while his brother returned to rule Albion. This, according to the *Historia Brittonum*, took place around 400 BCE and coincides with the sack of Rome by the legendary Brennus.

These works heap myths upon legends, co-opting the figure of Brennus – who may have been mythical even in the supposedly factual early history of Rome – and turning him into a king of the Britons. This is rather unlikely, to say the least, but by the time Geoffrey of Monmouth was writing the ancient history of Rome had become as wreathed in myth as the tale of the Trojan Wars.

At some point, Geoffrey of Monmouth's account ceases to be purely fiction. *Historia Regum Brittaniae* contains an account of the Britons' resistance to the Roman invasion of 54 BCE. Their leader is Cassivellaunus, whose existence is corroborated by Julius Caesar's account of his Gallic Wars. How truthful Geoffrey of Monmouth's account of the Saxon invasion might be is open to conjecture. He was drawing on the work of Nennius, who was more than a little biased against the invaders.

According to Nennius and Geoffrey of Monmouth, one of the chief opponents of the Saxon invaders was a Romano-British king named Ambrosius Aurelianus. After his death, he was succeeded by his brother Uther, who was known as Pendragon for reasons that are still debated. At this point the story veers back into mythology as the wizard Merlin helps Uther father a child who will become King Arthur.

The deeds of King Arthur vary depending on the version of the tale. Geoffrey of Monmouth has him discovering Iceland and conquering it, though that cannot have been difficult given that it was at that time unpopulated. After campaigning in Scandinavia and France, Arthur eventually subjugates Rome. This is all rather anachronistic; Geoffrey's Arthur seems to be active around 800 CE, at a time when Iceland had not been discovered and Rome was most definitely not the seat of a powerful state. Although it is utter nonsense as history, Arthur's conquest of Rome makes sense from a mythological point of view. Writing for an audience whose grasp of history would be rather slight, Geoffrey of Monmouth recast Rome as an easily identifiable opponent for Arthur. Readers would have a vague but powerful idea of the greatness of Rome, which suited the story Geoffrey wanted to tell. In this, Rome itself had become a mythological character.

Geoffrey of Monmouth's work founded the 'Arthur genre' which was added to and amended by later writers. The backstory he created tied the ancient kings of the Britons to the line of Aeneas and thus to the Trojan Wars, which in turn created a link to the Roman gods. Not content with claiming the kings of the Britons were descended from Venus by way of Aeneas, Geoffrey of Monmouth also threw in a line of ancestry going back to the sons of Noah.

These works influenced later writers, even after the questionable 'histories' were no longer believed to be true. Although not directly featuring Roman deities or mythological creatures, they tie in to the stories of ancient Rome. Indeed, King Arthur would appear to inhabit the same mythos as Apollo, Jupiter and the heroes of the Trojan Wars. If so, the sudden appearance of giants and other mythical creatures in the tales of King Arthur makes perfect sense.

KING ARTHUR WOULD APPEAR TO INHABIT THE SAME MYTHOS AS APOLLO, JUPITER AND THE HEROES OF THE TROJAN WARS.

Classical literature

Several of Shakespeare's plays are connected with Rome or Roman Britain. Four are generally considered to be 'Roman': Julius Caesar, Antony and Cleopatra, Coriolanus and Titus Andronicus. In addition, Cymbeline is set in Romano-British times.

Julius Caesar centres on a pivotal moment in Roman history; the assassination of Julius

Caesar. Fearing that Caesar would make himself a tyrant, the conspirators agree to murder him but fall out immediately after the deed is done. Thus begins the civil war that will eventually lead to Caesar's adopted son Octavian – also known as Augustus – becoming the first Roman emperor.

Antony and Cleopatra is set in the years following the death of Caesar. Mark Antony, one of the conspirators against Julius Caesar, has fallen in love with Queen Cleopatra of Egypt and is neglecting his duty as a military commander. He finds himself at odds with his former ally Octavian, and eventually meets him in battle. Defeated, the lovers flee and Antony attempts suicide, thinking Cleopatra is dead. He survives long enough to discover she is alive, in typically Shakespearean fashion, then succumbs to

BELOW: **An 1867 depiction of the assassination of Julius Caesar. Shakespeare's plays helped keep this event in the popular imagination, even among people who knew little about ancient Rome.**

ABOVE: **The Death of Cleopatra, painted in 1899 by Louis Marie Baader. 'Historical' images of this sort often contain anachronisms as a result of the painter's unfamiliarity with the period depicted.**

his self-inflicted wound. Cleopatra learns she is to be paraded in a Triumph and decides to take her own life.

These two plays are based on real events, but contain references to Roman mythology – at least, as Shakespeare envisioned it. Generations who have attended the plays or studied them in school have picked up fragments of Roman mythology and an impression of what the Roman world might have looked like, viewed of course through the rather distorted lens of an Elizabethan playwright.

Coriolanus is set in the early days of the Roman republic. It tells the story of a Roman leader who alienates the plebian class and is banished from the city. He presents himself to the Volscians, a tribe hostile to Rome, and agrees to lead them in an attack on the city. He is then persuaded to act as peacemaker between the two factions and is murdered by tribal leaders who are displeased by his actions.

Titus Andronicus differs from the other Roman plays in that it is a work entirely of fiction rather than being based on real events. The lead character returns from a campaign against the Goths, bringing with him their queen as a captive. What follows is an orgy of rape, murder and mutilation, characterized by misdirected vengeance and deception. The play seems to be an attempt to cash in on the success of similar bloody productions rather than having any historical accuracy.

Cymbeline is based on the life of Cunobelin, a British leader mentioned in Roman chronicles. It revolves around jealousy and plots within the court of Cymbeline and is only peripherally connected with Rome. Other plays include what might today be referred to as fantasy elements – gods, spirits and omens – which may well have been influenced by classical mythology. Shakespeare drew on the work of Plutarch and possibly other Roman writers including Livy for his source material, and would have been familiar with such concepts from his studies. This use

BELOW: Dante and Virgil in the ninth Circle of Hell, where traitors meet their eternal punishment.

of similar elements has contributed to a 'modern popular mythology' in which many people are familiar with all manner of divine and supernatural creatures but have little idea which came from what mythos, or which were invented to suit the needs of a play.

Some Roman writers have also become pseudo-mythological figures in their own right. The most notable is perhaps Virgil. The great Roman poet acts as a guide in Dante's *Inferno*, providing advice and explanation as he leads Dante safely through the layers of hell. Virgil is an ideal candidate for the role because he is a pagan and therefore cannot enter heaven, but he is wise, learned and cultured. When Dante is tempted to pity the souls being tormented in hell, Virgil reminds him that they are

receiving deserved punishment for their sins in life. This echoes the very Roman ideal of bowing to the will of the gods – be they pagan or Christian.

Modern literature and entertainment

A great deal of modern literature draws on Roman mythology, not always directly. The novel *Ulysses* by James Joyce is a modern interpretation of the heroic voyage, translated into the very ordinary lives of early twentieth-century people in Dublin. The grandiose myth counterpoints the trivial adventures of Joyce's characters as they make their way through the petty hassles of the day. The threats are much smaller – some verbal abuse and a drunken punch-up with a soldier – and the journey is much shorter, and overall the lives of Joyce's protagonists seem even smaller when compared with the great hero-myth. This is part of the genius of the novel, though its groundbreaking narrative style is sufficient for status as a masterpiece.

Other borrowings from Greco-Roman mythology are more direct. The animated television series *Ulysses 31* was essentially a retelling of the Odyssey as a science fiction show. Although the title and the name of the main character are from the Roman version, most other elements use the Greek names. However, Greek and Roman names were used interchangeably in some parts of the Roman world. *Ulysses 31* is littered with classical literature references and characters, with some episodes based very clearly on parts of the original poem.

Reworkings of Greek myths are popular among novelists and TV show writers, but Roman mythology is less commonly used. There are many who do not seem to know the difference, which arguably is entirely acceptable. Elements

BELOW: The novel *Ulysses* deliberately counterpoints the mundanity of its characters' lives with the ancient epic, creating a masterpiece of modern literature.

BY THE SAME WRITER

CHAMBER MUSIC
DUBLINERS
A PORTRAIT OF THE ARTIST AS A YOUNG MAN
EXILES

THE EGOIST PRESS
LONDON

ULYSSES

by

JAMES JOYCE

SHAKESPEARE AND COMPANY
12, RUE DE L'ODÉON
PARIS
1925

of both are interchangeable, and when creating a new work of fiction there is no requirement to stick to one single mythos. This can, however, cause confusion for those less familiar with the mythos in question – is Neptune the Roman sea god or the Greek one? Is Apollo a Roman or a Greek god?

Appropriations from Roman mythology – or of elements of Greek mythology that also exist in the Roman version – are sometimes less direct. Television shows and video games with a fantasy element often draw on mythological elements for inspiration or as a sort of storytelling shorthand. A magical weapon in the shape of a trident evokes Neptune and the sea gods; footwear or headwear with attached wings suggests a connection to Mercury and the power of speed or even flight. Sometimes elements are borrowed wholesale and without shame, with in-game equipment inventories listing Minerva's Shield or Neptune's Trident. On other occasions the inspiration is apparent but the developers have at least gone to the trouble of filing off the serial numbers.

In still broader terms, Roman mythology is one of the progenitors of the fantasy genre – along with the paranormal-adventure and arguably some forms of science fiction too. Encounters with monsters, magical dangers and the occasional deity are the stock in trade of such fiction. A starship encountering beings so advanced they seem like gods, or crewmembers landing on a dangerous planet, could easily be translated into mythology in the style of the *Aeneid* or the voyage of Ulysses.

The original and rebooted *Battlestar Galactica* television series revolved around a group of ships fleeing the destruction of their homes and seeking a safe haven. Echoes of the *Aeneid* are obvious. In one episode of the original

BELOW: **An elevator pitch for the original** *Battlestar Galactica* **movie and TV series might run something like 'The Aeneid, only with evil space robots'. The mythological parallels extend to names of characters and some situations encountered along the way.**

series the fleet had to pass close to a particular planet to avoid another danger. Their enemies had predicted this and built a powerful weapon there, perhaps reflecting the dilemma of Scylla and Charybdis. In the event, the crew of *Battlestar Galactica* were rather more proactive than Ulysses, launching a commando raid to destroy their Scylla. Whether or not this incident was inspired by Roman mythology, parallels can often be drawn in modern entertainment – after all, there are only so many plot elements in all of creation.

Likewise, many creatures of Roman mythology are staples of fantasy and sometimes paranormal-adventure fiction. Centaurs, satyrs, cyclopes, sea-monsters of various sorts are often relocated wholesale into modern fiction, along with nymph-like spirits that may or may not be inimical. Even where elements are not

MANY CREATURES OF ROMAN MYTHOLOGY ARE STAPLES OF FANTASY AND SOMETIMES PARANORMAL-ADVENTURE FICTION.

taken directly from mythology, the idea of incorporating them was established in these myths. The idea that the hero of a story might have special powers due to supernatural parentage is common in modern entertainment. These characters are modern-day equivalents of the demigods of mythology.

A military legacy

The Roman army was not the first organized military force of the ancient world, but it did leave a powerful legacy. The word 'soldier' comes from soldat, which translates as 'a piece of money'. This is because after the reforms of Gaius Marius, Roman soldiers were paid for their services in cash. In this they differed from the 'barbarian' warriors they encountered. Military service was at that time an obligation in most societies, with support

BELOW: **Many elements of the Roman army, such as uniformity of equipment and the use of regimental standards, set it apart from its 'barbarian' enemies and demonstrated concepts still in use today.**

ABOVE: **The instantly recognisable image of the Roman legionary is in fact a snapshot of a relatively brief period in the long history of the Roman state.**

and gifts offered by leaders rather than a regular salary.

The Roman army left an impression in other areas. Highly trained, well organized and uniformed, the Roman army served as a model for professional services of later years. Some of its symbology was co-opted, notably the eagle, which became the focus of a unit's honour during the Napoleonic era. The eagle was associated with Jupiter, who was of course the god of triumphs. Thus although he was no longer worshipped, Jupiter was still honoured on the battlefields of Europe.

The Roman army also left behind its own legend. Roman military artefacts are sometimes used by film-makers to indicate great danger lies ahead. The brave adventurers pass the site where a Roman unit made its last stand, or find Roman swords on a mysterious battlefield, and the viewer is tacitly informed of how serious the situation is about to get. The power and prestige of the Roman army, along with its instantly recognizable equipment, allow the film-maker to show that what lies ahead was too dangerous even for the finest of soldiers.

Of course, the popular image of the Roman army is itself something of a myth, given that equipment changed and evolved over time. However, the classical Roman soldier with his short sword and distinctive shield, crested helmet and segmented body armour has become part of modern popular mythology. Even some military experts fall victim to the mystique of the Roman army.

Some otherwise excellent works suffer from the fallacy that effective military operations require a uniform and a regular pay chest. The military skills of the 'dark ages' and medieval period are discounted as disorganized mob violence, and only

when a proper uniform is donned does competence reappear.
This attitude is less prevalent than it used to be, because the
different military environment of the post-Roman world is better
understood. Nevertheless, there is still a tendency to assign an
almost mythical status to the Roman army and to discount those
that came later.

Gods in the heavens

Nowhere is Roman mythology more prevalent than in astronomy
and space exploration. Constellations and galaxies are named for
Roman gods or mythological figures, as are most of the planets.
Mercury, Venus, Terra, Mars, Jupiter, Saturn and Neptune are all
named for Roman gods while Uranus is the odd one out – Uranus
was the Greek name for Caelus. Long considered to be a planet,
Pluto was downgraded to the status of dwarf planet in 2006.

Many moons and other objects are also named from Roman
mythology. In general, moons are given a name associated with
the planet (or dwarf planet) they orbit. Thus the moon of Pluto
is named for Charon, the ferryman of the dead who conveys souls
across the River Styx into the underworld. Likewise the many

BELOW: A third century
BCE mosaic showing the
seven stars of the solar
system at the House
of the Planetarium,
in the Roman city of
Italica. Each planet is
personified by a god.

moons of Jupiter are named for his lovers or offspring in Roman and Greek mythology.

The first western manned space programme was named Mercury, with connotations of speed and flight. Out of 25 flights, six were crewed. The Mercury programme demonstrated that short-duration orbital flights were possible and helped develop the technology necessary for longer missions. It was followed by the Gemini programme – named for the twins Castor and Pollux, because the Gemini capsule had two crewmembers.

The Gemini programme paved the way for the primary goal of the time – a landing on the moon. This was accomplished by the Apollo programme despite the tragic loss of three astronauts aboard Apollo 1. The first missions were groundside proving operations rather than spaceflights, but Apollo 7 orbited the Earth and Apollo 8 passed around the moon. The first landing was made by Apollo 11 and more followed, despite near-disaster when Apollo 13 suffered an explosion during liftoff. This has become the stuff of legends, but a less-known incident occurred to Apollo 12.

Slightly more than 35 seconds into launch, just as the rocket and its crew were experiencing the highest g-forces of the mission, Apollo 12 suffered the first of two lighting strikes, which disrupted critical guidance systems. Despite the extremely adverse conditions the crew were able to restore control and make a near-perfect orbital insertion before ultimately carrying out their lunar mission. The name Apollo was chosen for the moon landing project due to its connotations of archery, accuracy and wisdom. Perhaps if the crew had propitiated Jupiter, or even named their ship after him, they would not have had to contend with thunderbolts on launch day. Mythological names are still sometimes used for some space projects, whereas others are more directly evocative and media-friendly.

Roman mythology in art

Classical mythology is a popular subject for artists, and some images have become the standard depiction of mythological characters. Venus, sometimes with her lover Adonis, was painted by many artists including Titian and Rubens. The depiction of

OPPOSITE: **Many Romans would have been absolutely sure the lightning strikes suffered by Apollo 12 were the result of naming the mission for a god other than mighty Jupiter.**

the most desirable being in all creation gives an insight into standards of beauty at the time the works were created. Sandro Botticelli's most famous work is his 'Birth of Venus', depicting the popular version of her story in which she arises from the sea after the castration of Caelus.

Other great artists have tackled the subject of relatively minor characters. In 'Amor Vincit Omnia', Caravaggio depicts a nude Cupid lounging above objects symbolizing human endeavours – music, art, mathematics and literature. The implication is that love conquers all other pursuits and interests. The theme is also explored in 'Mars Being Disarmed By Venus', by Jaques-Louis David.

David also depicted courage and patriotism in paintings such as 'Oath of the Horatii'. He was working in a period of great turbulence, surrounded by the French Revolution and the rise of Napoleon, in which the values of the Horatii were greatly desired by those leading the revolution. David was among the most fervent of the revolutionaries, but also caused something of a sartorial revolution. His paintings were highly influential, and in many cases depicted hair and clothing in the Roman style. This in turn caused fashion-conscious French citizens to want to dress this way. Even furniture design was affected by David's work.

RIGHT: In David's 'Oath of the Horatii', three brothers swear to their father their devotion to victory even at the cost of their own lives.

Some renditions of Roman myth make rather less pleasant viewing. Among them is 'Saturn Devouring his Son', painted by Francisco Goya. Although such subject matter could never be light-hearted, the painting reveals as much about Goya's state of mind at the time as it represents mythology. This is always a factor, to some extent, whenever depictions are created from ancient myths. The subject is always filtered through the imagination and perceptions of the artist, which are influenced by the values of their time.

This in no way invalidates the depiction of a mythological character. The myths evolved and changed during the time they were the current religion, and Roman mythology would be viewed very differently by a citizen of 400 CE compared with someone from 400 BCE. A modern-day depiction of Mars might wear a flak jacket and carry an assault rifle without being less valid as a representation of the god of war. Indeed, such a representation might be more relevant to our world than Mars with spear and breastplate ... and gods must remain relevant or be forgotten.

ABOVE: Goya's depiction of Saturn eating his children was painted at a time when his native Spain had been wracked by the Napoleonic Wars, and reflected the painter's own dark state of mind.

Roman mythology in the modern world

Of all the mythologies of the ancient world, the Roman mythos is the one that has most influenced modern thinking and imagination. It was assisted, of course, by being so similar to Greek mythology, but of the two cultures it was Rome that left the greatest impression on the world. It is possible to view Roman myths as simple hijackings of their Greek counterparts, but this is not entirely accurate. Roman mythology built on and added to that of ancient Greece, notably in the way the *Aeneid* built on the Greek Iliad and extended the story. Indeed, it might be argued that Greek mythology owes its survival into the modern era to the Romans.

Some pieces of mythology have survived as references or figures of speech. Someone referring to the agent of their

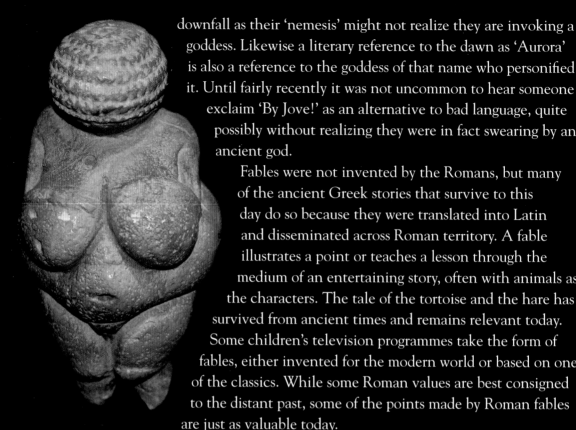

downfall as their 'nemesis' might not realize they are invoking a goddess. Likewise a literary reference to the dawn as 'Aurora' is also a reference to the goddess of that name who personified it. Until fairly recently it was not uncommon to hear someone exclaim 'By Jove!' as an alternative to bad language, quite possibly without realizing they were in fact swearing by an ancient god.

Fables were not invented by the Romans, but many of the ancient Greek stories that survive to this day do so because they were translated into Latin and disseminated across Roman territory. A fable illustrates a point or teaches a lesson through the medium of an entertaining story, often with animals as the characters. The tale of the tortoise and the hare has survived from ancient times and remains relevant today. Some children's television programmes take the form of fables, either invented for the modern world or based on one of the classics. While some Roman values are best consigned to the distant past, some of the points made by Roman fables are just as valuable today.

ABOVE: The Venus of Willendorf dates from up to 30,000 years ago, depicting an 'earth mother' figure which might represent the standard for a Venus of the time.

Sometimes Roman mythology resurfaces when an easy reference is required. Stone-age carved figurines apparently depicting a fertility goddess have been nicknamed Venuses, such as the Venus of Willendorf. Dating from around 28,000–25,000 BCE, this artefact cannot possibly have had anything to do with Rome or its mythology, but the label 'Venus' still makes sense. This was, it is thought, an object of veneration and represented a well-fed female 'earth mother' figure. Calling it a Venus created a simple and apt shorthand way of referring to all such objects.

An extremely difficult task might be referred to as Herculean, which would make little sense if the connection to Hercules and his labours had been forgotten. It may be that such references one day become merely words whose origins are unknown, but for now they add a richness to our language by their connotations. Describing a task as extremely arduous gets the meaning across just as well, but the Hercules reference is just that little bit more pleasing. Perhaps this is because in addition to conveying a meaning it evokes a good story, or perhaps we are still inspired by tales of gods and heroes. Thus Roman mythology survives into the modern world in many forms. Elements are borrowed for entertainment or advertising purposes and references are used in rhetoric. Language both crystallizes and influences thought, and although we no longer think in Latin we still make references to Roman concepts and ideas.

The effects on our thinking are difficult to estimate, because many of the influences are small or subtle, but what is certain is that the mythology of ancient Rome continues to exert an influence on modern society. While it continues to do so, the legends of Rome will never completely disappear.

LEFT: Hercules temporarily took on the burden of holding up the world from Atlas. Perhaps someday the story might be forgotten, but even so there likely will still be 'herculean' tasks to perform.

INDEX

PICTURE CREDITS